PRAISE FOR *SAINT THE TERRIFYING*

"*Saint the Terrifying* offers me—and you, Dear Reader—a day-pass to a world of pain, glory, lust, and limitlessness... [it's] deceptively ambitious..."
—Paul Wilner, *Zyzzyva*

"Two worlds collide head on, exploding across the page in glittering sentences that tell an eccentric and grimy vigilante story."
—Naomi Elias, *KQED*

"[A] heart-rending, beat-driven, often surreal voice."
—Jane Ciabattari, *Lit Hub*

"*Saint the Terrifying* is extravagant and interesting, sometimes rough, playfully dissonant, full of velocity... an inventive start to a bold new three-part saga."
—Anita Felicelli, *Alta Journal*

"Mohr writes with energy and a sense of music. Beneath the tragedy and neon mayhem runs a lovely optimism, a feeling of redemption and generosity toward mankind."
Steph Cha, author of *Your House Will Pay*

"Josh Mohr is a kind of punk rock arc-angel, and this wildly sacred book is on fire with his genius. It's everything. The whole horizon, within and without."
—Luis Alberto Urrea

"Delivering a pitch perfect voice, this is the book Henry Rollins would have written if he had been a fiction-writing-Viking, moshing to the Cro-Mags or The Misfits and viewing Sonny Chiba flicks, but he did not, instead you have the creatively powerful voice of Joshua Mohr at the height of his literary powers."
—Frank Bill, author of *Crimes in Southern Indiana, Donnybrook, The Savage* and *Back to the Dirt*

"Author Joshua Mohr's latest book is his grandest undertaking: It's a 1,000-page trilogy about a modern-day punk Viking named Saint...equal parts mosh pits, Norse gods and crime noir."
—Zack Ruskin, *San Francisco Chronicle*

THE WOLF WANTS ANSWERS

A VIKING PUNK SAGA: VOLUME 2

JOSHUA MOHR

THE UNNAMED PRESS
LOS ANGELES, CA

AN UNNAMED PRESS BOOK

Published in North America by the Unnamed Press.

www.unnamedpress.com

Unnamed Press, and the colophon, are registered trademarks of Unnamed Media LLC.

Paperback ISBN: 978-1-961884-41-0
EBook ISBN: 978-1-961884-42-7
LCCN: 2025932248

Cover design and typeset by Jaya Nicely

Manufactured in the United States of America by Sheridan

Distributed by Publishers Group West
First Edition

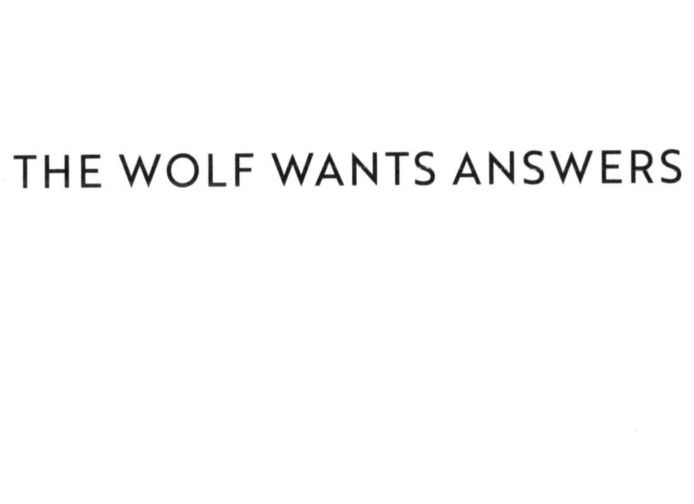

THE WOLF WANTS ANSWERS

PART 1

HAPPY MONSTERS

HEY, IT'S BEEN A MINUTE, you perfect ten, you pinup girl, you choirboy, you sacred cow, you whiz kid, you conniption fit, you does-the-carpet-match-the-drapes, you knee-jerk reaction, you joy huffer—

Wait.

Where was I gonna start this one?

Right. Yeah.

Thursday's gig.

The night when it all went sideways. The night of the hostages.

So sit back and listen, you cuck chair, you slow cooker tycoon.

Our band, All the Fuss, was on tour, playing Bottom Out in Phoenix. We—Trick Wilma, Got Jokes, Nameless Drummer, Dusty (our redeemed roadie), and me—were backstage, waiting for our cue to kick off. The signal came, the soundman flicking a switch, giving the stage watts. Yellow spotlights made the world look like nicotine teeth. Dusty wished us luck, and we rushed onstage like berserkers doing a hit-and-run raid. We were coming to town to invade bodies, shove aside vital organs, stash our music deep in their guts.

I wore only a pair of jeans and a pair of antlers painted fluorescent yellow. And since the club had a layer of smog from all the cigarette smoke, my reflective antlers cut through these fumes like lightning bolts. Our drummer got that kick spitting out a driving rhythm. For about thirty seconds, the bass drum was all that we heard in this scuffed Valhalla. Then most of those yellow spotlights cut out, save for one, framing Trick in a circle of mustard gas.

You couldn't see anyone else in the entire club.

Just that Valkyrie poet.

Just that pagan priest.

And then she hit the riff on her bass, had a sleazy, distorted tone to her rig. Kinda Lemmy. Kinda Matt Freeman. Each note she played cut through the murk, chugging from her amp, charging through the club's speakers, the ones that hung from the ceiling like schizophrenic elves.

We had the whole room on our side in ninety seconds.

Which was the entirety of our opener.

I knew the audience was on our side because of their singing mouths. They knew the words from our record. We'd done the whole thing in a two-day battle trance at some slum-studio in West Oakland. For $606.17.

Now people shouted the lyrics at our shows, like off-key rehab karaoke, and it was so batshit to watch them sing along, all of us in on it together, screeching our music of defiance. I couldn't stand still onstage, dancing through the mad weather of our songs.

For songs to be truthful, they needed to be covered in bruises.

Everyone in the club knew it.

Our giant electricity could handle the kiss of a star.

And I'm gonna hit the gas on the ol' broken baroque, let the language sound like a bouquet of grenades. Can I hand these violent flowers to you as a gesture of reckless love? Yes, let's lean down and sniff their blossoms together. Yes, let's pull their pins like we're plucking petals. Yes, I want our heads to explode.

As I basked in this bent joy onstage, a memory about a different concert, the only one I heard in San Quentin, a guard showing me a video on his phone—a big no-no on the inside—but he didn't care right then. He couldn't. See, somebody had sent him a video of his daughter playing in her piano recital and he needed to show anybody else, and I happened to be mopping nearby.

He held his phone and played the video, and he wept, which seemed an odd thing to do in prison next to a convict holding a mop.

"Isn't she wonderful?" he asked me.

That might mean that he was speaking about his daughter, this child he helped create, and so of course he found her wonderful.

Or it could mean that her playing was wonderful, which wasn't what I heard on the recording at all.

Or it could mean simply: *Can you even believe it's possible that we are here in a maximum-security prison, and somewhere else in the world an innocent girl plays the piano?*

"What's her name?" I asked.

"We call her Addy."

"Well, next time you see Addy, tell her I like her song a lot," I said.

For a minute, the two of us were together, before he remembered that he was a CO and I needed to finish mopping.

Now, back at the club: We stood onstage in the stunning pollution of the spotlights, and Trick spit an enraged chorus in the mic, the crowd screaming every word with her . . .

There could be maximum-security prisons and piano recitals in the same body.

YOU CHARISMATIC AMPUTATION, you vibrating bed, you debunked hypothesis, you pre-owned nervous system, you cheap Sphinx, you Chernobyl dog, you haunted wombat—and why were we all these grotesque violins whining at the sky?

Wait.

Right.

We left Thursday's gig and hit the highway, on our way to a brand-new club we'd play the next night. It had been a cowboy bar that some old punks recently bought. They were cool enough to let us show up and sleep on the floor, bathe in their bar sinks like gutter birds. It wasn't a glamorous life, but we didn't want to be anywhere else.

This was to be the joint's first week in existence, which might mean nobody showed up, but we were driving from Phoenix to Albuquerque anyway, and the gig was on the route. Even forty bucks in gas money would make it worth our time. I drove the Reliant east on I-10, dragging our trailer full of equipment. It was four a.m., and the desert was dark, and the windows were down, and the air had a taste of cumin, a hit of joy. My ears still rung with the voices singing with us from the crowd.

Our drummer didn't come with us; he'd met a girl who had the time off work, and they were going to have sex across the Southwest, as they had put it. We'd see them at the new club, though of course we'd beat them there. We were already close.

This stretch of road was empty. Trick was in the passenger seat next to me. In the back, Got Jokes and Dusty were twacked on acid and malt liquor, playing Uno. Not playing so much as holding their Uno cards near their fried mugs, moving them gently up and down, like crazed geishas fanning themselves.

"I mean, shit, yes," Dusty said, "if you have a Wild Card, man, that's . . . wow. I mean, a Wild Card? That's like holding the Bible. That's the good Word. That's the great permission slip in the sky. That's Allah giving you a cardiac arrest and bringing you back with math."

"You're nudging me toward a panic attack," Got Jokes said. "Is that your intention with this line of thought?"

"Anything you can do with a Bible," said Dusty, "you can do with a Wild Card—that's what I'm saying. You want the whole world to turn red or blue or yellow or green? You just say it. You speak it and ooh-la-la. Poof. Say it and amen. Mazel tov. The world's red. And you did it, you minister, you medicine man."

"I have some Wild Cards in my hand right now," said Got Jokes, "and I don't want the pressure. Who am I to turn the world red? Who gave me that kind of authority?"

Dusty stopped fanning himself with his cards. "You shouldn't tell me what you have. Uno is a serious sport."

It had been a while since either of them had played a card, just clutching them close to their oily faces, staring at each other with their fun-house eyes.

"That's not to mention the black heart of Draw Four," Dusty said to Got Jokes. "A Draw Four is like giving your mother an atomic bomb for Christmas."

"I just said I couldn't handle the Wild, man," Got Jokes said, "and you're dropping Draw Fours on me? You're talking atomic bombs?"

"There is a whole stew of meaning out there. I mean a whole stew," said Dusty. "That's all I'm saying. These things mean things."

Got Jokes nodded. "Totally, these things mean things, yeah."

Dusty shook his cluster of Uno cards. "The answers are frightening. Welcome to the macerated facts of the twenty-first century. Nothing can be trusted. But we need to keep our eyes wide open."

"Yeah, well, I'm doing the opposite," said Got Jokes, and closed his, still with the fan of his Uno cards close to his face. "I'm keeping mine closed until the atomic bombs are gone. You should try it, too, Dust. It's peace in here behind my eyelids. Out there, I see too many bombs. But there's peace inside."

Dusty shrugged, shut his eyes. "Hey, I see it! There is peace in here! I didn't know what peace even looked like, and there it is!"

Peace had that in common with pornography: You knew it when you witnessed it. I watched them in the rearview. Their four eyes shut. Got Jokes nodding placidly. Dusty smiling, saying now, "Who knew all you needed to do was take acid and shut your eyes, and you could meet peace?"

Then they both passed out, and it was Trick and me, in our longship, floating across the ocean. "I dig these shows so much," she said. "It's crazy that they sing the songs with us."

"It's so crazy," I said, and what I meant by that was the same thing Addy's dad meant when he showed me her recital in Quentin—except I was the one in the video.

"Take the next exit," Trick said. "Just a few miles till we're at the club. The last stretch of road is dirt."

"A dirt road," I said. "Always a harbinger for a packed house."

"All I care about is that soon we'll dump these idiots off, and I'll let you go down on me," she said, and leaned across the seat and grazed me on the neck with her tongue. Then she said, "See that exit? That's us."

I pulled off and followed the map we'd written, and this was the last part of our instructions: Stay on this ribbon of road for four miles, and once you were convinced that there was nothing here, drive another mile, and that was when you'd find the club up over a rise.

The road was still paved, but I could see ahead where it turned to dirt. It was a straight shot. I hadn't bumped the wheel once.

We left the paved surface, and I kept the Reliant revving at a solid forty-five down the dusty straight lane.

No lights, except the beams from the Reliant's bow.

Suddenly, there was something lying on the road in front of us.

I saw it too late to brake.

I couldn't swerve, or we'd crash into open desert.

We'd flip for sure.

So I kept going straight.

The Reliant ran over something barbed, its teeth puncturing the tires, tearing them to black confetti. Car went wild, tires squealing, bucking this way and that, skidding, as I tried to hold the wheel steady; the trailer on the back was extra weight to negotiate now, felt like we were going to flip over to the right and then it felt like we were going to flip left, but once I got us straight again, I took my foot off the accelerator. We stopped rolling in about fifty feet.

Our acid aficionados didn't stir in the back seat.

"What did we run over?" Trick asked me.

I didn't answer, throwing open the door and jogging back till I spotted what slashed our tires.

"A spike strip!" I told Trick, returning to stand next to her open window. And because I now faced the dark road ahead of us, I made out a hulking black vehicle blocking it, some kind of armored truck by the looks of it. Three figures stood next to it in the road. I peered more closely as they stepped into the farthest reaches of our headlights.

A koala.

Princess Di.

And Beetlejuice, whose hands looked zip-tied.

I was supposed to be lying down with Trick, not dealing with costumed freaks. The koala held a cigarette in his paw and smoked with the outrageous enthusiasm of someone staying straight in rehab. Princess Di stood in the middle of the three and adjusted his junk under a pink ball gown. Zip-tied Beetlejuice, on the other hand, stood perfectly still.

Trick followed my line of sight, then said, "Who the fuck are those cosplay assholes?"

"Don't know yet," I said.

"Should we fuck them up?" Trick asked.

They weren't moving, only standing carefree in front of the armored truck. I didn't know if they had weapons. All I knew was that I didn't, so I'd have to do this hand-to-hand, man-to-man, even if one of them was dressed like Princess Di.

"Lemme go ask if they have AAA," I said.

"I'll come, too, in case you get confused on the spelling," Trick said, climbing out of the car and standing next to me. There were perks to loving a Valkyrie. It was grand to share important events with people you loved. Maybe you played Scrabble or pickled veggies. Not us. We fucked shit up. After a quick kiss, we put our hands in the air, showed empty palms to the masked assholes, and walked their way.

As we did, we got an idea, and not a good one. No, this was one of those mad maneuvers, one of those near-impossible notions you entertained for a beat before dismissing its sawdust potential. There was no in-between with this idea of ours, no, only the poles, the binary, live or die, and the berserkers in my blood cheered us on, and they wore wolf faces like crowns, fangs out, telling us how many times they'd sprinted into oncoming arrows and spears, howling, mouths pointed to the moon, and they didn't care about anything except this one animal moment, so we began our charge.

"That's far enough, Nancy!" Princess Di screamed almost immediately. The voice confirmed a man under the costume with an Asian-sounding accent. "You are Nancy, right?"

I stopped dead in my tracks. Di had called me Nancy. How could he know that name? Trick, now paused as well, turned to me. "Nancy?"

There was no way to explain it to her, given the circumstances, and so I made the one suggestion I could: "Start the charge."

"Music to my ears," Trick said.

We sprinted, yelling war sounds, speaking in the tongue of combat.

Still, none of them moved.

Were they bait, pulling us into the kill zone? It didn't make sense, them standing statue-still with two lunatics bearing down.

We were almost there.

I was a cathedral made of adrenaline.

I wanted to slow dance with a tsunami.

I wanted to plug my guitar into an electric chair.

The lousy koala had another cheerful drag from his smoke, and the disrespect made me livid. Didn't he understand that we were coming for blood?

"You take Beetlejuice," I said to Trick.

I'd hit the koala first, an overhand, then a knee to his stomach. He'd be flattened, and I'd headbutt Princess Di, dismantle the face through the mask, a nose in eight pieces, eyes watering so badly he couldn't see the moon. A blood choke if necessary to finish the job.

We were eight feet away.

Two steps.

Two seconds.

I was one fist already coming back.

I was another hand up to protect my face.

I was a hive of ancestors.

I was a wolf who wanted answers.

And that was when Princess Di ripped the mask off Beetlejuice's head.

That was when I saw who was underneath.

I SCREECHED TO A STOP, inches from the three of them. Trick did, too. I gasped for air, not understanding what I was supposed to do now that I could see the face under the mask. It wasn't a man standing there in the striped Beetlejuice costume. It was Cassidy.

I smiled, and she screamed at me: "Don't do anything crazy, James! You don't understand what's going on, so don't be fucking crazy!"

"James? Who the hell's she?" Trick asked me.

"Two steps back now!" Princess Di said to us. A skinny prick, this one. Hitting him would be like fighting a child.

"What if I don't want to move?" I asked.

"Be a touch careful," said Cassidy, using the inside joke from our past life.

But she knew I didn't know how to do that.

So Trick and I didn't move back two steps.

"Nothing else can happen, Nancy," Princess Di said to me, "until we know you're going to stay calm—and you begin by taking two steps back."

"These sound like orders," I said, not moving. "Is that what's happening? You're giving me orders?"

"Just a touch careful," said Cassidy to me. "Please."

"Saint, tell me who she is, goddamn it," Trick said.

We didn't move back two steps.

"We are humble couriers," said Princess Di to me. "Nothing more. We are not soldiers, like you. We don't want to get bloody."

"Don't sell yourself short," I said. "You did lay a spike strip down, almost kill my friends and me."

We didn't move back two steps.

"We are humble couriers *and* spike enthusiasts," Princess Di said, then he spoke to Cassidy: "Tell him what you know."

Cassidy looked at me, really looked at me. This woman who swore we'd never see each other again, not under any circumstances. And so I had put her on the pyre in my brain, burned her away. Now she was right in front of me, incarnated as a zip-tied Beetlejuice.

Being alive meant we caught ghosts in our hearts like fish in nets. I pointed at her costume. "Très chic," I said.

"We're in deep shit," she said.

"This will be over soon. We can have breakfast and catch up."

"I'm going to punch you in the face," Trick said to me.

Then Trick punched me in the face.

"Can you wait a minute," I said, "before hitting me again? We need to figure out what's going on."

"I can wait thirty more seconds before hitting you again," she said.

"What's this arrangement Princess Di's talking about?" I asked Cassidy.

"They know the two things we love most," she said. "They have my brother—and you know what I did to get him back. They also know what you love more than anything . . ."

She didn't have to say it. My happy monster.

“I’m sorry,” I said to Princess Di, “can you tell me whom should I be speaking to? You and her? This is confusing.”

“Take two steps back,” he said, “or the deal is over before it starts.”

“Good. I don’t want a deal,” I said.

“You owe a debt, Nancy,” said Princess Di, “and you will pay it.”

“I owe a debt to you?”

“We are humble couriers,” he said. “You owe a debt to our employer.”

“I’m not taking two steps back, and if your employer wants to talk to me, why isn’t he—or, sorry, she—here right now?”

“Please stay calm,” Cassidy said to me again. “I’ll never get my brother back, and—”

“And you,” Princess Di said to me, “you’ll never get your guitar back.”

“We have his guitar, asshole,” Trick said.

“Do you?” Di asked, laughing behind his princess mask. “While you talk to the left hand, the right hand works. This is something the courier knows.”

I spun and sprinted back toward the Reliant, to the trailer attached to it with our gear. Trick sprinted with me. The lock had been cut, dropped in the dirt. The doors were wide open. The way we always packed the trailer, the drums were by the door, so I climbed through the metal jungle of cymbal stands and toms, knocked shit all over the place in my haste, getting toward the back where my rig and the happy monster slept. The case was gone.

No case, no guitar.

I thrashed my way back out of the trailer, toppled cymbals, crashing their tinny noises. I shoved our amps against the wall, impressed that someone had slid through this gauntlet without making a racket. I spotted my antlers sitting on my cabinet, and they knew the time for language or reason was no more. It was time for teeth.

I rounded the corner, coming up on the Reliant's body, and Trick said, "So we fight?"

"We fucking fight."

Then the first gunshot took out our right headlight.

The second, the left.

Trick and I stood in the dark.

"Never mind," she said to me.

"Now, Nancy," Princess Di called from somewhere in the black, "do we finally have your full attention?"

We were talking in the darkness.

Like after lights out in Quentin.

Absolutely pitch in our cells.

We lost all our muscle and were disembodied voices.

And I'd like to tell you about one night specifically. I heard an old cellie crying. It happened more often than we wanted to admit. Sometimes, if you listened close in Quentin, you could hear someone's mind break, and the man screamed all night like his brain was in a bear trap.

You had to *work* to keep your shit together. I started each day the same: with my own fist hitting my jaw. I started by saying out loud to my dead father, that coward who cut his throat, "I am not going to kill myself today," and then I hit the floor for a thousand push-ups.

The cellie I'm telling you about—he wasn't hysterical. No, he was doing his best to cry quietly in the dark, and that made it worse.

We were on our bunks, stacked one on top of the other. We couldn't see anything.

"What is it?" I asked the crying man.

"Just something I heard."

"You're crying about something you heard?"

"It's about a monkey."

"You're crying about a monkey?"

"He was like us. This monkey was locked in a cage for twenty-eight years. In a research facility, which is just code for a concentration camp. He was born in captivity and never went outside, not once, in his whole life."

Men were more honest in the dark. That was something I learned in there. When we could see one another, we didn't know how to stop thumping our chests. But once it was lights out, cons could unload all kinds of blues.

"He never went outside?" I said. "That's why you're crying?"

"I'm not crying because he was locked up for so long. We know lots of guys who will never get out. I might be one. I'm crying *because* he got out. He served his monkey sentence, and after twenty-eight years, they moved him to one of those sanctuaries where the animals get to live the good life."

"Happy ending," I said.

"Forget the ending. That's not what we're talking about. What I'm saying is he's never been outside. Do you know what that monkey has never seen if he's never been outside?"

"What?" I asked.

"The sky," said the crying man. "Motherfucker had never seen the sky in his twenty-eight-year life."

He'd been cooling down, but that last line made my cellie start weeping again. We didn't get to pick what ruined us, what broke our lewd hearts. He probably never expected this monkey to mean so much, but he couldn't get the image out of his head, couldn't unsee this moment, the first time the animal walked out of a building, tilting his head up toward the clouds, the sun, the birds. This monkey must have thought he'd died, must've wondered how in the hell life could show you splendor after such cruelty. This monkey might philosophize: *Would the sky have looked so majestic to me without the twenty-eight years locked up? Was it that long malice that made the sky shine?*

My cellie and I had already been whispering, and our voices got even quieter now.

"You might get paroled," I said. "It's not impossible."

"Nah, they won't let me out, and they shouldn't."

He was right about that. Civilization was better off with him in here. But that didn't mean I couldn't cheer him up right now.

"What do you think he thought?" I asked.

"Who?"

"What do you think the monkey thought seeing the sky?"

"He thought, *Shit, that's been up there the whole time! Who the hell kept this from me?*"

"I don't care what you say—I think you're gonna get paroled," I said. "I think we'll both be outside again. And we can go to the drive-in movies. Stargaze while giants act on-screen."

"If I ever get out," he said, "I won't see a movie or watch TV again. I don't want any of that canned noise. No, it's only real life. Real life all the time."

"Real life all the time," I said.

"He saw the sky," he said. "After a life in a cage, the monkey saw the fucking sky."

M

Back to the dirt road in New Mexico right after they shot out our headlights. Princess Di and I were two voices yelling at each other in the darkness. We had no bodies anymore.

"Cassidy will fill you in more," Princess Di said, "on paying your debt."

"If I decide to pay," I said.

"Do you want to get your guitar back? What you call your 'happy monster'? I was led to believe that it was invaluable to you and that you would do anything to retrieve it."

"Including coming to find you."

"We are humble couriers."

"You are humble couriers and dead people," I said.

"You really are a mad dog, aren't you?"

"You never said whom I owe this debt to," I said. "Is your employer that scared of me?"

"On the contrary," said Princess Di, "he sought you out, remember? You will meet when you arrive."

"Arrive where?"

Princess Di laughed. "You will meet when he wants."

"So he is scared of me."

"Real gangsters move in the darkness, Nancy," said Princess Di. "You should try it sometime."

"I'm a Viking, not a gangster—and we fight in the light."

Footsteps, doors opening, an engine sputtering, headlights igniting. The armored truck turned toward us, not trying to hit us, but passing close, too close. They sped by us on the road's edge, heading back to the highway.

Then the dirt road was quiet.

After a few seconds, I heard coughing out in the darkness.

"Cassidy?!" I said.

The coughing quit, and nothing for a few seconds. Then, without answering me, the crunch of boots coming toward us. Could she really be back from the dead?

I was down a happy monster. And up some kind of debt.

"I want fucking answers about her right now," Trick said to me.

Cassidy wasn't close enough yet, just ghost crunches in the dark, so in this moment, it was still just Trick and me, All the Fuss, and we were on tour, playing her songs and the new music we wrote together, and we had plans to gig in front of as many kids as we could, wanting to hear every one of them sing along with us.

But that wasn't gonna happen.

Cassidy would be here any second.

PART 2

WATERLOGGED GHOSTS

(EIGHTEEN MONTHS EARLIER...)

WE MET ACCIDENTALLY, when I was right out of lockup, in the time before I was called Saint and before I knew how to drive.

I'd taken BART to Civic Center, walked up Haight Street from Market; I could've hopped on the 7 to charge the hill on Muni, but I wanted to wander, to marvel, to feel gratitude at the dirty poetry popping off around me. I had come here fresh from living in a concrete village filled with apex predators, and I craved the openness of the streets. It was almost noon, a chowder sky with a potato-white sun concussing anyone dumb enough to look up.

Soon, I'd be up at Mom Jon's, nabbing my Tele and playing that happy monster till my fingers slobbered blood. It would feel so righteous, this pain from my music. See, in Quentin, I had to endure my finger calluses fading, and I hated those forgetting fingers, felt them going smooth, soft. My songs were leaving me. In prison, it was impossible not to dwell on what you'd squandered. Even something as simple as calluses on the tips of your fingers could wreck you.

I trekked Haight hill, walking it because I wanted to, because I could. No guards or gangs. No cages. I was going to get a box of Pop-Tarts. Frosted cherry. My favorite. I needed to remember living in this before life. I pictured the old neighborhood. The Lower Haight before it went and got all swanky while I'd been away.

On the corner used to be a good mom-and-pop shop. Soul food. Fried fish sandwich so greasy you might propose to it. May even be able to cop a couple grams in there, if you knew the right name, if you were so inclined.

I was not inclined any longer; those days were behind me.

Which was a stupid expression. Everything was behind us. Even the future. That was why it always snuck up. And sometimes the future kissed you, and other times it left you weeping on the floor.

Next up on the corner of Fillmore and Haight was the Walgreens where I worked when I was seventeen. My job was mostly to "face" the shelves, meaning to pull products right up to the edge, so it never looked like anything got bought.

It always looked like we had it all.

Over there, that used to be a punk rock café. Back then, one of the ladies slinging caffeine had two straight razors tattooed on her jawbones, their handles by the ears, their blades meeting at her chin. I always wanted to kiss her.

Now, the café was gone, replaced by a boutique where you could buy suitcases carved out of gold boulders.

I also remembered a great Ethiopian place up the block that made its own honey wine. I sat there with my aunt, Rebecca, before she died, and she'd sneak me sips of that sweet juice when I was underage. Not like we needed the buzz. We were already licking our morphine lollipops.

I kept walking, and the neighborhood kept coming alive with all these memories, these ghosts, and please don't think that I didn't know the truth: I was a ghost, too.

I was a little worried about seeing Mom Jon when I got to her place. I looked back on living with her with pure affection. She and Rebecca gave me something I couldn't imagine after my father killed himself. I never thought I'd ever feel welcomed again, and there was Mom Jon and her Victorian and her dirt stage for the poetry readings, showing me that just because Tron was gone, it didn't mean that I was. I ruined that, of course, the drugs piloting my senses like suicide bombers, but those first couple years were righteous.

Like most, Mom Jon wrote to me more at the beginning of my bit in Quentin. I understood. I fucking judged her silently, but I understood. It was hard to keep up correspondence with a murderer.

I hoped to explain it all to her. Apologize. Then I'd make the happy monster shriek. I'd press my fingers so hard on those strings, making them remember, chord by chord, calling those calluses back from the dead.

But a funny thing happened as I walked up and stood in front of Mom Jon's old, condemned Victorian.

Would you like to hear this funny thing?

The old, condemned Victorian wasn't there.

Huh.

Nope.

New condos.

Wait, were they condos?

I had an untrained eye. I'd heard the word *duplex* tossed around a time or four but wouldn't be able to pick one out of a lineup with other bourgeoise geometries.

But lucky for me, this fancy house still had enough in common with the working class to have a front door, so I marched up the five stairs. Grabbed the knob. Locked. Looked inside: A lobby filled with balloons.

So many balloons, the whole room was a celebration, and way off on its other side, there was a woman screaming on the phone, cussing somebody out. I could see her body but only through the reds and yellows of the balloons, ribbons, those drugstore umbilical cords, hanging down to the checkered floor. She was furious, yelling verses of profanity.

I knocked on the door, waved. I tried smiling, but I barely remembered how. I was rusty at being alive. I heard her say into the phone, "I wish I could give cab fare to a bear who'd come to your office and maul you, Tony!"

To be indirectly greeted in a very San Quentin cadence made me like her immediately. It was so casual and so mean and so beautiful, her unique hallelujah as she swam through a jungle of balloons, shoving them out of her way, the ribbons sticking to her face, her hair. But about three steps from the door, she stopped walking, gazed down, took a deep breath. She was around forty, wearing a black dress patterned in sunflowers. She had carved arms like a warrior's. I knew something was off with her face, but, for whatever reason, I couldn't immediately put my finger on it.

She took a few more deep breaths, then, beaming, threw open the front door, apparently excited to greet me. "My first! They say you never forget your first!"

My head was cocked, studying the riddle of her face.

"It's the eyebrows," she said. "Dumbass."

Yes! That was it. I had no intention of disparaging the eyebrow-less, only saying they were gone. I wanted to reassure her that I wasn't being a prick, so I tapped on my glass eye, said, "I also suffer in the eye region."

"Right, great, I'm a huge asshole, thanks," she said.

"No, I think you're great," I said. "I liked hearing you yell at Tony, whoever that is."

"I lost a bet with him," she said, "so I lost my eyebrows."

"He sounds like an asshole."

"Sorry about calling you a dumbass," she said.

"So what were you talking about when you opened the door? I'm your first what?"

"This is my first listing, and you're the first to visit," she said. "I'm a new real estate agent, or I'm trying to be. Honestly, I have no idea what I'm doing."

She needed some encouragement. "The balloons are a proper touch."

"Two hundred of them. I went overboard. I'm nervous. Shit. Sorry. I still can't believe I called you a dumbass. I've never had a normie job before. I'm trying. Who cares about all these balloons if I'm insulting the customers, right? Like I said, this is my first time, and I'm mad about my eyebrows. Fucking Tony."

"I've been known to go overboard, too," I said.

"I'll get even with him," she said. "Believe that."

She waved me inside, and I followed her into this balloon grove, the colored bubbles bouncing off my head as I followed her through, colliding with these little planets, these little parties, zooming through a lobby-galaxy.

Yesterday, I was in a San Quentin cage, and now the universe was made of balloons.

"It must've been important," I said.

"What?"

"The bet. To risk your eyebrows."

"It was Tony's idea," she said. "I can't believe I let him do this. I want to blame him, but aren't I getting too old for that crap? It's me. My fault. I'm like you. I'm a dumbass, too."

"He shaved them?"

"Right on my big day with the listing. He's the one making me become a real estate agent. I work for him. I shouldn't complain. I used to work at Subway sandwiches. I came home covered in rashes from handling all those embalmed meats. Nothing makes you want to kill yourself more than being covered in a Subway rash."

I told a lie of solidarity: "I like Subway."

"It's not that I feel like a failure. It's that I don't know how to forgive myself for being one. Do you have any idea how much worse that is? Look at me, talking like an old lady."

"You're not old."

"When you reach my age," she said, "your whole head feels like a tombstone. Listen, you're young, so you can rest on the feather bed of your dreams. Every sad fuck in their forties and fifties and sixties, they gotta live with their failures. Most of us, those feather beds of our fluffy ambitions vanish, and now we know the truth: There are no feather beds. Everybody sleeps in the dirt."

And now I didn't need a lie of solidarity. I needed the truth. "I've slept in the dirt my whole life."

"Whatever happens to you in the future," she said, "promise me you'll never take a job at Subway. I swear, the rash on your arms will look like Freddy Krueger's face."

Was there a way not to fall in love with this woman?

"Back to Tony," I said. "If you work for him, why would he want you to sell the place without your eyebrows?"

"He says he's helping me."

Another balloon bounced off my face. It was clear to me that Tony was the sort of man who should be beaten unconscious, but it wouldn't do any good to tell her that. No, she didn't need my threats of violence. She needed a compliment. "You're lucky," I said. "You have the kind of face that doesn't need eyebrows."

As soon as it was out of my mouth, I regretted its nonsense. *You have the kind of face that doesn't need eyebrows?* In addition to being rusty at being alive, I was double rusty at giving compliments.

"I don't believe you," she said. "Everybody needs eyebrows."

"They're overrated."

She told me her name was Cassidy, and she led me to the elevator. A couple of ribbons had curled around her arms, and she dragged balloons behind her like floating severed heads. "You know the real tragedy here?" she asked. "This isn't my first Tony. Tonies, I shit you not, grow on trees."

"Tony trees?"

"Far as the eye can see," she said. "Poisonous groves of Tonies."

The small elevator arrived, door squeaking open. It, too, was crammed with balloons, say fifteen of them. We got in and could barely see each other.

"You didn't tell me what the bet was," I said.

"I can't. It's embarrassing. But I mean it this time. This Tony shall be held accountable. He'll be my effigy to all them Tonies who have wronged me."

When we hopped off the elevator, she herded all the balloons into the hallway, and we walked to Unit 12.

"I'm going to say something," she said, "but it's lame, so don't laugh."

"Okay."

"So I was thinking I'd tell each person as I opened the front door for the first time, to really get them excited to see the property—I'd say, 'Welcome home.' Do you like that, or is it silly?"

"Who doesn't want to be welcomed home?" I said, remembering my first breath out of Quentin. Even oxygen felt different in there. State-issued. Cut-rate.

"All right, here goes then." She opened the front door, held it wide for me, and said, "Welcome home."

How long had it been since somebody had held a door, had smiled, at me?

Welcome home.

That was what she said.

The door opened onto the condo's kitchen. The whole place was staged and had that Ikea ick. Cassidy pointed to a tray of shrimp with a bowl of cocktail sauce on the kitchen counter. "I wouldn't eat any yet," she said. "They're still icy in the middle. Nobody wins with a shrimp-sicle."

No dearth of eyebrows or semifrozen shrimp could sully hearing something so hopeful come from her: *Welcome home.*

She said it, and I heard it.

She didn't mean Mom Jon's, of course. She didn't mean the condemned Victorian, with our dirt stage in the living room where we'd have those poetry readings with the old snapping hippies. She didn't mean me taking care of Rebecca while she was dying, before she hopped off that bus and disappeared.

No, Cassidy meant this new condo. They'd razed our Viking village and built a Christian shrine. But I wasn't upset with Cassidy about that; she didn't buy the place and tear our house down personally. Whomever she worked for, however, might be able to point me in

Mom Jon's direction. "I actually used to live here," I said, "so, in a way, you are welcoming me home."

Her face went sour. It took a few seconds to spackle that charm back on. "Does that mean you're not here to buy? That's totally fine. I like you. I just want to know what I'm dealing with."

"Guess I'm not your first after all," I said.

"Good. I can finally pee."

"Sorry I didn't level with you right away."

"You did look too young," she said, "but in this ridiculous city, hey, maybe you're some start-up millionaire asshat."

"I'm an unemployed felon."

"Ah, I remember those days."

"I'm looking for work," I said. "I got out yesterday."

"Stay away from Subway," she said. "They'll hire anyone there, and you'll have a rash before your first paycheck. Just go right into real estate. They'll let any hustler do this shit."

"I didn't know the old building was gone," I said. "I came here to see my friend and pick up my guitar."

"Oh. I'm sorry." She thought for a minute. "If you want to take all the shrimp when you leave, go ahead. They'll thaw in an hour or so. That way, it's like I'm buying you lunch. It's the least I can do after calling you a dumbass and trying to sell your old house."

She was a person, and I was a person, and you were here, watching us, peeping Cassidy, who picked up that tray of shellfish and held it out to me, and it was the only selfless thing anyone had done for me in years, and it was in a moment like this that I realized joy was just circumstances, context. I'd seen a thousand trays of shrimp in my life and none of them meant anything, and this one blew my heart up like one of her balloons.

She turned me into a happy monster, which made me remember that I was here for my Tele, and I knew that I needed to turn my attention to that, and it was gonna happen soon, yes, definitely, no doubt, I'll get to that, but hold on, hold up, give me a minute drenched in these northern lights.

"That's generous," I said to her, "but I want you to keep the shrimp. I want you to sell this house today. And maybe some shrimp lover will walk in, and this will seal the deal."

"Are you sure?"

"We can make a trade, shrimp for information."

"That might be the oddest suggestion anybody's ever made to me," she said, "and I spent a summer smoking crack and following Butthole Surfers around the country."

Then the intercom rang: Someone was downstairs wanting to see the place.

"Okay, so if I keep the shrimp," Cassidy said to me, "what do you want to know? Shrimp for information and all."

"How can I track down the woman who used to live here?" I asked.

"There's only one way," she said, "and unfortunately, he's named Tony."

CASSIDY GAVE ME THE LOCATION of Tony's office on Taraval Street, some stucco slum-shack out by Ocean Beach, jammed between a taqueria and an Irish bar. Most real estate offices I'd seen were swanky, polished, but this place was pink gray, the color of ham turning—and coincidentally, Tony brandished a similar pickled hue.

I hopped off the L right in front of his office. As I entered, I saw there was only a desk with a globe on it in the center of the room toward the back. Besides that, there was a big aquarium running along one wall.

Tony sat at his desk and was hooked up to an IV. Some junkie paramedic monitored it. This vampire had cooked himself on the night shift and its mad medicine. He hadn't slept in a thousand years. He'd sold his bones to pawn shops. The vampire paramedic flicked the IV bag and hummed a tune, PJ Harvey's "Meet Ze Monsta."

I stood near the door, waiting to be acknowledged.

"Closed," Tony said to me. "This establishment is closed for hangover maintenance. Once I've got a clean bill of health, we'll open right up and be our best self."

"Cassidy sent me," I said.

Tony pointed at the humming vampire, still tapping the IV bag. "I pay him handsomely and he shoots me up with vitamins," said Tony, "and I'm right as rain. Hey, maybe that's what these vitamins are made of: rain." He laughed, too hard, then he said to the vampire, "I think I can hear it raining in me."

"I'm looking for a missing house," I said.

"Can you hear it? Is it raining in me?" he asked the humming vampire, but all he did was shrug, hum, tap another fingertip against the bag.

Tony turned his attention back to me: "We are closed until further notice."

"Cassidy said you could help me."

"Hangover maintenance."

"You're a prick, huh?" I asked.

"Sit. Relax. Nap. Leave. Flee the country. Jog in place. I don't care. We're closed until further notice!"

So I stepped close to Dracula's perverted nephew and used a bit of the Quentin charm on the paramedic—"Take the air or take a beating"—and he stopped humming and scooted from the office.

I gripped the IV, pulled up on it just enough so the needle threatened to rip out of Tony's arm. This, realistically, was not that big of a deal. I wasn't going to rip it out. It was just some pressure. But he didn't take the pain well, this yelping pickled man. To say he was a pain baby would be an understatement.

I held the tubing in my fist now. I wasn't going to do it. Of course. For one, this man was a coward. He wore it like cologne. The way his eyes went wide looking at the needle that hadn't even torn through the skin, you'd think he'd been speared right in the heart, the pain baby. He was looking around for the pearly gates, miracles, his insurance card.

I could leverage his absurd panic.

And could, maybe, even have a couple laughs along the way.

"You would lose a lot of blood," I said, tugging gently on the tubing, the needle.

"That's what I was thinking."

"A proper gusher."

"Would you call 911?"

"You'd have to earn it."

"How?"

"By telling me what I want to know," I said, and gave another tug, this one harder, sure, but not rip-it-out hard. I was being good. I wasn't getting busted back.

"Tell me what you need to know!" he said.

"I need any information you have on Mom Jon," I said, and gave him her old address, her full legal name. I leaned in very close to his face, made direct eye contact, tugged at the needle again, pulling on his chicken skin

"Can I go over to my computer?" he whined.

I nodded, let go of the tubing. He got the intel on the quick, a few taps on the keys, and I held a page with her forwarding address. I didn't see a traditional addy listed. No, instead it only said "Slide City. Montake, California."

"That old waterslide park?" I asked. "The one where those kids—"

"The one and only," said Tony.

I had a map to get the happy monster back. Too bad it was leading me to that waterslide park, a cursed place. This was also going to require some liberal interpretation of a few California laws and statutes and other slangs of bureaucrat blah-blah. Because I was due back at the halfway house by sundown each day, there was no way I could make it to Montake and back, which would only be a problem once I figured out how to get out there. I could pay for a lift. It would be four hours, round trip. Maybe tomorrow, if I faked a full day of job interviews, I could get there.

But I wanted to get to Mom Jon and the happy monster today. I needed to play that Tele, needed to hack and slash my music. I needed to know that I hadn't lost it in there. You didn't come out the same. That was impossible. If I didn't play music soon, I was gonna rage.

As I stood in this swirl, I found another way to scratch the itch, turning my attention to Tony, to Cassidy, to the mystery of her eyebrows. He still sat at his desk.

"What was the bet?" I asked him.

"What?"

"The eyebrow bet with Cassidy."

"It's complicated," he said, and I said, "We're only talking, and talking isn't complicated at all," and I walked to him and grabbed the tubing, pulled up on it, stressing the needle in his arm with limited force. The pain baby didn't disappoint with his aggrieved reaction. He was on the threshold of full-blown blubbering.

"Is it somehow feeling less complicated for you now?" I asked.

"Okay, okay, I bet her a hundred grand that she couldn't sell that house today without eyebrows."

"That doesn't make sense. Why?"

"She couldn't win."

There was another world where another man named Saint stood in this office and heard those words, and that Saint did the right thing—or the thing that was justice to me—yes, the right thing being the one you'd do if we were allowed to live lawlessly, without rules or oversight, and that Saint yanked the IV needle out of Tony's elbow crease and planted it right into his biceps, then his neck, finally planting it in Tony's cheek. Yes, this freethinking, heroic Saint from another universe brought his face down close to Tony's stuck cheek, and Saint said to him, *You are a cruel plant that needs to be drowned in pesticides.*

I, however, couldn't behave like that Saint, whose name I did not yet inhabit. And certainly not here. Not with the stink of Quentin still working its bleach from my pores. Tony didn't deserve my violence, even if he was an eyebrow-shaving coward, though I reserved the right to remix that opinion.

"Why couldn't she win?" I said.

"I'm not saying shit."

That other Saint pulled the needle out of Tony's cheek and stuck it right in his ear, and it sprayed blood. Sweet Jesus, that other Saint was a mean son of a bitch.

He was not, for the record, a lucky son of a bitch. That was for sure.

He was mean, which I wasn't.

My Tony was fine, even though he shouldn't have been.

Do you see how levelheaded I was?

I was merely a tugger of tubing, not a ripper of it.

"If you choose not to answer," I said, jiggling the needle in his elbow crease, "you're going to get blood on your clothes."

"Look, we're dating—and she's not easy. It's been a rough couple weeks. I was teasing, I guess. Getting even, maybe. She's hard on me. Has a temper. She's mean. It's only her eyebrows. They'll grow back."

"So you did it to be a dick?" I asked.

"No. Yeah. I don't know."

"You shaved her eyebrows for no reason?"

"I said I don't know."

"You're not telling me why she couldn't win."

"I can't say anything else."

You'd need to know violence like I do to spot the slight tweak in his demeanor. Yes, he was already scared in this moment with me. He understood I could hurt him; however, his preexisting fear pulled at him, like it had a line and a needle in him, too. There was something or somebody who scared him more than I did.

That Saint from another world was laughing his ass off at this prospect, pointing right at me, calling across the galaxy, "Are you gonna let him get away with that? I thought we were Vikings!"

Some Saints had all the luck.

I shuddered at my strange restraint. Maybe I only needed a former Subway employee. "If you don't tell me," I said, "I'm going to sic Cassidy on you."

He shrugged, looked away from me toward whatever scared him more. This was new for me. I was usually the scariest person. We'd need to do something about that.

I kept picturing Cassidy from earlier, furious in that garden of balloons in the lobby, screaming at him on the phone. And I kept hearing her say he wasn't her first Tony. And I kept imagining how cruel the world must have seemed as her eyebrows hit the floor. And it was supposed to be her big day. And yes, he tried to take that away from her, and yes, she wanted to buy me lunch, a tray of shrimp, while he was sitting right here getting an IV of rain.

Plus, I really liked how she looked in that sunflower dress. Plus, she needed a new man.

You were only rusty at being alive until you weren't.

I was going to give her a gift named Tony, which technically would require a slight breaking of the law, but only a little. He wasn't going to be harmed in this speck of crime. No, it was just some old-fashioned chair cinching until Cassidy could get here.

SHE KNOCKED ON the front door. No one could see Tony tied to the chair from the street. I'd put the Closed sign in the window, shut the blinds, and turned off the overhead lights. It was about five p.m., the fog bombing in from the beach.

I'd also left him here unattended for a brief stint so I could hoof to the liquor store for Pop-Tarts, and I ate the entire box. One after the other. I devoured them, right on the street, and I found myself smiling again, the sugar made me alert, the socked-in sky made me hopeful, and I had a huff of joy, one, two, three, breathing it in.

Now I said to Cassidy, as she took in the scene, "Well, you sure were right about Tonies. This guy is awful."

"Tonies give my pussy cottonmouth," she said.

He looked at her with hurt, gaspy feelings. Tonies, in addition to being the worst, also possessed dramatic knacks.

"That makes sense," I said.

"I have a couple questions for you," she said to me, "and let's start with the whole tied-up thing."

"I only did that after he confessed," I said.

"For my eyebrows?"

"I tied him up for you."

"You can get in a lot of trouble for this," she said.

She was right, of course. A day out of lockup. It wasn't ideal timing. But I was never very good at walking away when people were being taken advantage of. The idea that this worm could shave her eyebrows, play his mind games, cheat her, never get held accountable—nope. I would always help.

"Hear me out," I said to her.

"It doesn't matter why. You can't tie people up who don't want it."

I decided to hose Tony's secrets down so she could peep his filth. Maybe if she heard the whole story, she'd understand my position: "He lied about your hundred grand," I said to her. "He knew you'd lose the bet. You had no chance."

"Why would he want to shave my eyebrows?"

"He said he did it to get even with you."

"To get even with me for what?" she said.

"He said you guys fight a lot."

"He tricked me into shaving my eyebrows because we fight a lot?"

She took a minute to gaze at these shivering naked secrets. I would've given anything to know what twinkling malfunctions went off inside her. I wished to climb into her heart like it was a punk club so I could hear the boiling songs.

"I'm changing my mind," she said to me. "Thanks for tying him up."

"And he'll tell us why you couldn't win," I said. "He'll stay tied to that chair till he does."

Then she stormed right up to him. "You know how much I need that money. I can't believe you'd lie about that." She fought back tears. "That money is how I get him back, and you lied to me. Made me walk around that open house all day looking like a no-eyebrows idiot. And I bought fucking balloons!"

"Balloons?" Tony said.

"Shut the fuck up," she said, suddenly busting up, hysterical. She leaned over, slapped her knee. "At first I thought I wanted to shave your eyebrows, too, but they'd just grow back. I want to destroy something you hold dear."

There was a head-scratching pause where it seemed everyone was stumped about what Tony might hold dear. And then he caught her gaze, and I did, too.

She was smiling in the direction of his aquarium. "I'm going to shit in your fish tank," she said.

"No!" he said. "I got forty grand of fish in there!"

"No mercy for an eyebrow shaver," she said.

"But I love them," said Tony. "They're like family!"

"Correction: You've got forty grand of fish family *and* my shit in there," she said.

An audible gasp from Tony

Cassidy marched over toward the aquarium, climbed a folding ladder, daintily opened the lid, and turned so that her ass swayed over the tank's surface. "Fish live in the ocean and people go to the bathroom in there all the time," she said, "so your forty-grand fish will be fine. But I want to ruin what your aquarium is, your little ocean. You're a tiny man playing God."

I knew this moment had nothing to do with me, but I couldn't help myself. She inspired me, as corny as that sounded. She compelled me to interrupt. "Hey," I said to her, "what are you doing tomorrow?"

I could tell she wanted to get on with her business defecating in the tank, but she took the time to answer. "I'm definitely not working for this guy anymore, so my day is now free."

"I want to take you to a probably haunted old water park," I said.

We stared at each other.

"Are you asking me out?" she asked.

"I am."

"Even though I'm about to—"

"Shit in a fish tank, yeah," I said.

I wished those lobby balloons were back between us, reds and yellows, everything alien and optimistic.

"I'd love to go to a probably haunted old water park with you," she said.

Then she put her game face on, shook her arms out. She put her hands on her hips, poised to hoist up her sunflower dress. It was go time, baby. Time for her to prove a point—one that, perhaps, only she could comprehend—but sometimes that's enough. Sometimes, it doesn't matter if others understand why you need to shit in a fish tank.

But right before she did, Cassidy said to me, "So we preserve a little bit of mystery for our first date, you might want to see yourself out."

THE FOLLOWING TRANSMISSION came to you live from Planet Halfway House, a distant world made of loony bins and beautiful rubble. A two-story shitbox painted entirely brown. Thirty of us in five bedrooms.

Its rep wasn't dangerous, and that alone made it more inhabitable than Quentin. Still, there were too many men sleeping stacked up, bunks running five to the floor. We were on top of one another, and no one wanted to get busted back, so we all had the same plan: play by the rules, get out of here as fast as we could. But it was clear we all still had hair triggers. Nobody was soft.

I'd just attended the show-up-or-serve-time AA meeting, and now I could cross "See a Neo-Nazi Cry About His Childhood" off my ex-con bingo card. Right after the meeting, the house manager marched me into the kitchen and introduced me to Python Wally. My job that night was dinner prep. Wally even had a couple inches on me, standing about six-nine. He had a blizzard-white ZZ Top beard, wore it jammed in a hairnet. Tufts of wonky beard spilled out, like pubes from the bathing suit of an old woman.

The kitchen was a blast of bleach up the nostrils. A room perfumed with so much of that toxic hygiene that it made my eyes water.

"These motherfuckers live on minimum wage," Python Wally said to me, as though our meeting had been planned for months, "and the least we can do is serve them the meatloaf on time."

"Yes, I agree," the manager said to Python. "That's why he's here, to help hurry the meatloaf production along."

"That's fantastic news," Python said back, smiling like he'd snorted a line of that Miami electricity. "I need a meatloaf man, and this big fella can certainly handle the assignment." He looked me in the one eye, and we had a proper stare-down. Python Wally was real, would get bloody without a second thought. He said, "Do you have any meatloaf experience?"

"Some," I said, which was true. I'd enjoyed it many times.

"How are you with confrontation?"

"I'm a Viking," I said.

Python smiled and clapped. In that second, we both decided we were gonna get along fine.

"A Viking," he said. "Yes, that's what I want to hear. You can be my meatloaf man any day of the week."

And ten minutes later, my hands were in rubber gloves, and I was kneading a trough of ground beef next to someone called Python Wally. He led by example, and I appreciated that; he, too, was elbows-deep in meat.

Now three of us wore hairnets: me, Wally, and his beard. My mohawk was smushed, the liberty spikes flattened out.

We listened to Otis Redding on the radio.

"Why 'Python'?"

"It started as Albino Python Wally, but people found that too lengthy."

"Before it was shortened, did they call you Albino Python because you're big, white, and mean?" I immediately lost interest in the question because I looked down and saw that he wore flip-flops with socks. "People shouldn't wear flip-flops except to the beach," I said.

"I wear them in days ending in *y*," he said.

We talked shit, kneaded the beef. Python showed me what ingredients to add, and then we shoved the troughs in the oven. While we waited for them to brown, he got us two Mexican Cokes, the real ones, made with sugar.

We cheers'd to our first meatloaf, a job well done.

He said, "But you're thinking about this all wrong." He held up one of his socked, flopped feet and shook it around like a prop. "They're a disguise. They disarm people. Nobody is afraid of some flip-flops pussy."

"And then you show them that you're an albino python."

"Flip-flops are like a Trojan horse. On your feet."

"No," I said, "I don't think that's right."

"The good news," he said, "is that tonight is our writing class, and attendance is mandatory."

ᛗ

This wasn't the writing class you typically pictured. Not a college workshop. Nobody had a monocle or wore elbow patches, though plenty of us had our elbows tattooed. No disgruntled white undergrad boys from the suburbs in Che Guevara shirts writing sob stories about boarding school. This was a conference room in a halfway house, the walls splattered with motivational sayings: REACH FOR YOUR DREAMS! That kinda tripe.

But I wished these posters told the truth. I wished there was one that had a smiling piece of dynamite, and it had little dynamite arms and hands, and it held a little lighter, the flame flicked on and close to its own fuse, lighting its own little dynamite world on fire, and the caption STOP RUINING YOUR LIFE.

On the far wall, there was another poster with a galaxy on it that read BE FAR OUT!

"'Be far out'?" I said to the guy next to me. "Is that a saying people say?"

"'Be far out'?" he asked.

"Yeah."

"First I'm hearing of it," he said.

The teacher walked in and quieted us right down. An old-timer. Black sweatsuit. Jordans. Been through the fire himself, you could see that in how he caught your eye.

"It's Maurice's last day with us," the teacher said, "and you know what that means."

I did not know what that meant, though they filled me in. The teacher helped each student work on an essay about their life, their bad times, whatever they needed to process. Apparently, he and Maurice had written five drafts of this piece together, and now that Maurice was leaving, it was time to read it out loud to the group.

"I have a surprise for Maurice," the teacher said. "I sent it to a friend of mine who runs a literary magazine, and they're going to publish it."

"How much cash?" Maurice asked.

"Zero cash."

"Do they sell these magazines?"

"They do."

"For money?"

"That's usually how it works."

"So someone not named Maurice gets paid for these magazines," Maurice said.

"Now you're catching on."

"Everyone has their hustle."

"Congratulations, Maurice," the teacher said. "It's one hell of a read."

"Have you ever been published?" Maurice asked the teacher.

"Pleading the Fifth," he said, then addressed the group: "Some of you don't know Maurice, depending on how long you've been with us, but he's turned into a solid writer. It's a very personal piece, a lot of pain in it, and I want to thank Maurice for reading to us. He's a brave motherfucker."

Maurice walked up and stood at the front of the class. "Don't laugh, assholes."

I wanted to say something encouraging—*Be far out!*—but Maurice was turning serious, and I settled in.

This is the story he told us:

"Fishin' up in that Arctic—did a season on a hellhole boat, barely running when we said good riddance to the woes of dry land. We were out to sea with plenty of food and plenty of whiskey and plenty of spliffs and pills. Worked hard during the day, and we plenty'd all night long, became boozy friends. Only things that worked harder than our aching bodies were the gasping bits in the engine. The captain was a felon who stayed at sea as much as possible and couldn't care less if an engine gave out. He'd simply be in the ocean, free, not a care in these seas. But we were navigating icebergs, and we took a big hit from one up front, more water coming on than we could bail. We couldn't care less, wasn't our boat. All this meant was a day without work. We radioed it in. They knew right where we were. Three hours till they scooped us up, they said. *Take your time,* we wanted to say. We got the food, the booze. We disembarked for some jolly iceberg shore leave. We were ecstatic sailors tearing ass into port. Music played on someone's phone. We watched the boat sink like it was a Hawaiian sunset. I remember cracking a fresh bottle of whiskey, sucking from it, feeling vacation-y, and looked out at our surroundings, admiring the peace.

"Then I saw the bear.

"You peep them on those nature shows, and their coats look so white, perfectly white, and they trollop on the snow with big, floppy feet, and maybe you even think they're adorable animals.

"But not if you're seeing them ground level, no, like that, they look alien. Too gigantic for this planet. It doesn't make sense that we're here and they're here. We're just chum to those space-traveling monsters.

"I'd estimate it was about a half mile off, maybe thirty icebergs between us. It stayed on all fours but stretched its neck to a preposterous length, like a periscope, and it did some gigantic sniffs into the air.

"Then it strutted to the edge of the berg.

"Then it roared.

"Then it dropped into the sea.

"We didn't have anything except knives and a rifle. Twenty gauge. Single-shot action. We had shells, which we immediately counted. Twelve.

"We had six men, knives, one rifle, twelve shells.

"Versus.

"A fucking polar bear.

"It was a hunter from the rip. Slow. Methodical. These were the bear's waters, and we were meat. It went under the water, and all I could think of was what should I call this bear? Doesn't make sense to me still, but being around a bear makes you think crazy things. It felt important to name it. Felt like it needed a name, because I knew as soon as it went into the ocean that it was going to be a crucial part of my life story. I knew I might be eaten alive—that was a real possibility—and so allowed myself this silly pleasure of naming the bear Jesus Christ.

"Let me tell you this little-known fact: It was impossible to tell time while the bear was under the water. You couldn't keep track of the seconds. You didn't know how fast Jesus Christ could swim. Was he about to shoot up onto our berg and slaughter the six of us? Would it be now? Or now? Now? No fucking way this moment could listen to the clock. This was bear time, goddamn it. This was teeth and bonesaw jaws.

"And it was under the surface still and a century went by and an eye blinked and a child was born and a fireworks show photobombed the sky, and the bear finally climbed on the berg right next to where he first went in the water. He'd made barely any progress. Roared, sniffed the air again, went back under. He was playing with his food.

"And that was what the bear did. He tortured us. One berg at a time. Getting closer. We had six men, knives, one rifle, twelve shells. We started arguing the right distance to begin taking our shots. Twelve shells felt like a fair chance to hit the bear, though we had no idea what kind of damage it took to topple Jesus Christ.

"Slowly, it was coming, and we decided that we couldn't take the chance that, as the bear got closer, it might make a dash for us, so we reasoned to fire about eight bergs away. One of us, Shaw, learned to shoot in the army, and so he took the first shot. And missed. I didn't know if this bear had ever seen a gun before or not, but the predator seemed to understand that perhaps the situation had changed with this new metal twig. This time, the bear didn't strut toward the berg's edge. No, this time the beast hurried. We'd threatened him. And we all knew in our own ways that we were about to die. Rapture by bear. Jesus Christ coming to our lonely berg to end our suffering.

"Again, I tried counting seconds, but the numbers had no meaning, no code. I was just making noises. It had to be three minutes with the bear underwater. Three! Shaw reloaded the gun. Some of us held knives; the rest brandished broken bottles. One man had taken off his sock and jammed it into a half-drunk bottle of vodka, aiming to throw a Molotov cocktail at Jesus Christ if the opportunity presented itself. The rag was soaked, and he had a lit cigarette in his mouth, ready to light the bear up.

"But what we learned is that you only thought you were ready to face a bear. We huddled toward the middle of the berg, back-to-back-to-back, gazing in every direction. And faster than I've ever seen something move—I don't even mean for its size—I mean the polar bear sprang out of the water, and in four quick steps, it hit one of us across the face, clamped on to his leg, dragged him into the water before we could do anything about it.

"We wanted to believe that we were people who shot or knifed or Molotov'd a bear, but when the moment came, we weren't up for it.

"Panic. An argument. Some thought there was enough time for Shaw to get off a shot. We were turning on one another. The stench of self-preservation was in the air. We all doubted our weapons. What, he was gonna toss vodka at a *wet* bear and try to light it on fire? What, we were going to try to stab a polar bear while it swung claws at us with longer, stronger arms? What, Shaw knew how to hit a moving target, one that was attempting to kill him, with a shot? We weren't ready, weren't brave. We were simply humans dropped onto an alien world, one with a monster who kidnapped our friend. If our fear kept multiplying, if it all kept on this way, pretty soon, we'd be heaving our pals into the ocean to save ourselves.

"Jesus Christ parked our friend on the next berg over, dragged this screaming man to the middle. Then Jesus ate our friend alive right in front of us.

"It wasn't what I saw. No, we all turned our backs.

"It was what we heard.

"And smelled.

"The smell went inside you.

"He took his time. Made him a proper meal. We all contemplated saying something, as we waited our turn to be murdered. This was the end of our lives, and somebody should say something about that. I didn't know if people eulogized themselves or not, but it seemed better than nothing.

"We all took a bottle and were gonna give ourselves a self-wake. We were going to drink to our health, our life, our death, rest in peace or power or feed the worms or feel the fire. Conjure the face of somebody you'd loved, remember the heat of how their fingers fired you up. Think about warmth and maybe something corny about your folks—anything was fair game when you were minutes away from being devoured by a bear.

"Also, we needed to get good and loaded. If you were gonna get eaten alive by Jesus Christ, get liquored up. You couldn't be numb enough, with the polar bear coming.

"We novocained our bodies with booze, and we tried to make our peace with being ripped apart. It was no longer a concept, death, no longer an abstraction, a mirage off on the horizon. It was a real place that you could only see when it was here, death, and these last seconds of your life were the hell I always feared them to be—destitute, these fucking seconds, stripped of any currency because there wasn't enough of them left to amount to anything, to mean anything. There wasn't enough time to make good on all those IOUs, the collection agencies in our brains. Oh well, we knew it was coming, death, it was almost here, death, and none of it mattered now anyways. None of it would be remembered. We wouldn't be remembered. Our great-grandchildren wouldn't even know our first names. We were cold, and there wasn't enough whiskey to deaden the terror of being eaten alive.

"Then we heard the spinning blades of a fat angel approaching. A helicopter. It got close, hovered, fired on the bear a few times, missed, and Jesus Christ disappeared in the water with a stomach full of a friend of mine."

And we all sat rapt, listening to Maurice read to us, and he was a person, and I was a person, and you were a person, and we were all with him in the Arctic, on the berg, flush with whiplash, one minute knowing that your destiny was to be gobbled up, but suddenly a song saved you—the music of the helicopter blades—and you were going to survive. It reminded me of being in prison, which was a planet of polar bears, a world made of shivs and batteries in socks and metal mop handles turned into weapons, fights to the death. Each cell was an iceberg, each man never knowing if today was when he'd be pulled under.

M

The next morning, Cassidy picked me up at the halfway house. Our first stop was Tony's office. He was still tied to a chair, which we can agree was his fault. All he had to do was tell us the truth, and he'd be free—free to fish the turd out of his fish tank, for starters. But a Tony is gonna Tony. They never make things easy, these Tonies.

"Are you ready to answer some questions?" I said, as we strolled into Tony's office. "Who's the new owner of Mom Jon's place?"

"All I can tell you," he said, "is that it was bought by a corporate investor."

"Does this corporate investor have a name?"

"Corporate investors are companies," Tony said.

"Companies have names."

"It doesn't matter."

"It matters to me," I said. "Somebody's going to live there, right? So who's that?"

"I'm done talking," Tony said.

"My job is to make it matter to you as much as it does to me," I said. "You're probably not going to like this part."

"You wanted to know who bought the place and I told you," he said, showing more defiance and heart than he had yesterday. We'd see how long he held up when we gave him some low-grade breakfast torture. Now, what was breakfast torture?

"You're right," I said to Tony. "You did tell us about a corporate investor, and that deserves a reward."

We'd brought him a shawarma, seeing as how he hadn't eaten for who knew how long. Why were we feeding him a shawarma in the morning? Because nobody wanted that, and we hated him.

"I'd like to do the force-feeding honors," Cassidy said, peeling half the shawarma from its paper. She fed the log to him, not always waiting until he finished chewing his current bite before shoving the shawarma back in. I got the sense she was super enjoying this, an intuition that was immediately confirmed when Cassidy said to me, "I can't stop shoving it into his face, and it's great."

"I get that," I said, "but please don't suffocate him with a shawarma."

She thought for a minute. "Fine, I'll pull it out if he goes red."

I got down close to him. My nose grazed his. "What do you know about Norse mythology?" I asked.

He didn't answer me, which was fine considering the shawarma and all.

"Can you at least make some noises so I know you're listening?" I said.

Tony let loose a series of frantic babbles that lasted about ten seconds, then Cassidy said to me, "He's going red."

"Seems to be."

"I guess I could pull it out for him," she said.

Tony nodding and nodding and nodding, the best suggestion he had ever heard.

But I wasn't ready for him to be sans shawarma. "Not yet," I said to her, and then said to Tony, "I asked what you know about Norse mythology. Don't you think you should answer me?"

He gave a trill of shawarma sounds.

"Baldr," I said to him. "The god of light, peace, forgiveness. He had a dream that he would be murdered. Since his parents were gods, his mother insisted that everything from the entire Nine Realms vow never to harm her child. Frigg was her name, and she carried so much weight that all existing matter pledged devotion. Of course they wouldn't hurt Baldr. Every single thing in the world promised that loyalty, except mistletoe, but Frigg had so little regard for the plant that she didn't consider it a real threat. That was all Loki needed to hear, that mad rascal. Those shitty Marvel movies have taken the balls from Loki, but he was a real Viking, conniving and bloodthirsty—and because of that, Loki made a spear with a tip of mistletoe and killed Baldr."

"Whoa," moaned Tony and the shawarma.

"You got that right," I said.

"He's really red," Cassidy said, nabbing the sandwich from his maw, holding it even though it had drool running down its squat length. He gasped for air.

"How did you know that Cassidy wouldn't sell the condo?" I said.

Tony licked at the corners of his mouth, flexed his jaws in big circles. "I can't tell you what you want to know," he said.

I gave Cassidy the signal, and she jammed the shawarma back in his mouth.

"Thanks," I said to her. "I'm having a good time with you."

"Me, too," she said.

We smiled at each other like shy kids at a junior high dance as Tony looked on with a shawarma half sticking out of his mouth, and I wanted to kiss Cassidy but didn't know if I should, and I felt myself flush—rusty at being alive and all.

"I need to finish up with him," I said to her.

"I can't wait," she said.

I said to him, "I wasn't done with my story, Tony. Baldr was murdered, and he is the god of forgiveness. Someone took from him—and he's able to rise up, he's able to absolve. But he's a god. We are not. He's better than us. I despise what you did to Cassidy. So you don't deserve any forgiveness. And maybe you're saying, *Okay, great, but what's the point of what this lunatic's saying?*"

I grazed our noses again.

He was going red again.

I had a huge balloon of joy again.

"I need a day job, Tony, and since Cassidy quit your shop," I said, "you just hired me to fill the position."

And he nodded his head *yes yes yes yes yes yes*.

"You hired me full-time. I need work coverage at the halfway house so I have my days covered—so I can go find Mom Jon."

Yes yes yes yes yes yes.

"And I need an advance on my salary. Call it a signing bonus. Five thousand."

Yes yes yes yes yes yes.

"Finally, you're going to tell me why Cassidy couldn't win the bet. There's something off with this corporate investor shit. I'm going to figure it out."

And he shook his head, grunted, "*No no no no no no.*"

"You're going to do it because you don't want to stay tied to that chair."

Still shaking his head *no no no no no no*.

He talked behind the shawarma, meaning he wanted it removed.

Cassidy ripped it out of his mouth.

"These guys are killers," he said.

"What kind of Viking would I be if I was scared of a corporate investor?"

"An alive one," Tony said. "I'm not saying anything else."

Since he was done talking, we did the only civilized thing, sticking the shawarma back into his mouth and watching him turn red, though we pulled it out before he went unconscious.

"It's this simple," I said to Tony. "If mistletoe can end a god, what do you think I can do to you?"

TONY NEEDED some time to himself to ponder his options. We left him in his chair to think, though we helped him finish his food, guzzle some water, and hit the head before we tied him up again.

Then Cassidy and I drove out into the East Bay. The temperature pushed eighty already, the sun deciding it should be the only thing in the sky, the bully. We were on our way toward Montake. Slide City. Toward Mom Jon and, hopefully, my happy monster.

Cassidy wore a dress patterned in ferns. She drove Tony's car, an eighties Corvette.

"Hey, do you like the Cramps?" she asked.

"Very much."

She turned up the stereo.

"Since we're on a road trip," I said, "do you want to be Thelma or Louise?"

"I'm whoever got her pussy licked more."

"I don't think they had that kind of relationship."

"Oh, please," said Cassidy, "every woman is a lesbian on a road trip."

We went over the Carquinez Bridge, sped past an In-N-Out Burger every other mile, and were soon into farmland: almonds, grapes, pavement, sprawl, dust.

I hadn't talked to a woman outside of the workers in Quentin in years. I hadn't been in a Corvette with a woman in my whole life. The contrast was too brutal. Like going from a funeral house to a greenhouse, death to life, a revived Viking, and the music was loud and the Cramps were rockabilly cool, and I wanted to stand on the roof of the 'Vette, wanted to take off my clothes, wanted the wind to hold me up, wanted to know: Should we stay up late tonight and watch a meteor shower? Should we paint the town, walk the dog, shoot the duck, save the cat, cut the cheese? Should we whisper our secrets, and could you sing me to sleep as the sun came up?

Sorry.

I was rusty at romance.

Cassidy kicked off her shoes. "I like driving barefoot."

"I've never tried it."

"When you take your shift behind the wheel, give it a go."

"No, I've never driven a car," I said.

"Why not?"

"My father taught me to ride a motorcycle as a boy. But I've never driven a car."

"I'll teach you," she said. "It always breaks my depression when I'm helping people."

It surprised me to hear her talk about depression so casually. Years back, I was diagnosed as bipolar in county and never told anyone. "You don't seem depressed to me," I said. "I mean, you did shit in the fish tank. Depressives don't usually have that kind of energy."

"Thanks for saying that," she said. "I'm the kind of depressed where all I want to do is shop for boots and masturbate."

"One of the things I dig about you, Cassidy, is that I never know what you're gonna say next."

"You'll appreciate this then: I have a sneaking suspicion that I was way kinder before my boob job. I looked it up on the computer, to see if there are other cases, other women, like me, who got new boobs but also a huge attitude. But I couldn't find anyone else like me. Which I guess is a compliment? But a lonely one, if that's a thing. A lonely compliment. *You're the only boob-jobbed lady in the world who lost her kindness. Congratulations, Cassidy.*"

She did that two-hour drive in one.

ᛗ

We found Slide City off an overgrown access road, about ten miles from the closest freeway exit. They weren't maintaining this stretch of road, after what had happened here. Years back, this had been a destination for high schools having end-of-year days at the water park. Then a bunch of kids clogged one waterslide on purpose, as a prank, using their bodies to make a kind of dam in the slide's middle, and they were all inside, about thirty of them, and as I tried to picture it, I was sure they were having a kickass time in the tube, laughing their heads off, must have been; they were these invincible warriors who knew that no matter what they did, nothing could bring them down, stampeding into their futures with confidence and airs, on top of one another in the slide, and it echoed with laughter, so loud, and they didn't know anything was wrong, didn't know how badly their body weights were about to rupture a hole in the slide's belly. By the time they realized they were in danger, they were all skydiving, falling a hundred feet down, no survivors, all lost for something so silly, so inconsequential—*Let's jam a waterslide as a joke, how hilarious!*—and suddenly you were flying, falling, a million memories bombing your brain in this descension, your cinema with its swan song screening.

These kids were in the sky, and then they were not.

I was living with Rebecca and Mom Jon in the Lower Haight when it happened. It was big local news. The park was sued out of business.

Now, we pulled into the parking lot. Totally empty, cracked, unmaintained. From the looks of it, no one had been here in years.

"Let's go up close," I said to Cassidy.

"This lot is where I'll teach you to drive."

"You don't have to do that."

"I want to," she said.

The old waterslides were dinosaur skeletons—a family, maybe, grazing, minding their own business, and bam, that asteroid hit.

There was a wire fence running around the entire Slide City. We pulled the Corvette right up front and parked by the old ticket windows.

"Let's look around," I said, and we got out, walked straight to the front gate. I could feel the Vikings huff a little joy in me, that old itch, approaching a new village.

That thrill of the unknown.

That thrill of the massacre.

We went right up and pressed our faces to the fence. I scanned the sky and found the slide that had the hole, funneling those kids to their graves. I wondered if I went into that slide now, if I climbed this fence and walked into that big, dry throat, would I still hear the laughter of those dead kids?

"Should we hop the fence and look around?" Cassidy said.

To be a gentleman, I turned around while Cassidy climbed over.

"You're sorta old-fashioned, aren't you?" she asked.

"I don't think so," I said. "I tied up Tony."

I jumped the fence, and soon we were to the turnstile, both walking through it. It was silly but also sort of fun, like we were dumb customers coming for the slides. We walked by the locker rooms and a bunch of overturned tables and chairs. There used to be a snack bar here, but it had burned.

"He's not in danger," I said. "Tony. I won't hurt him. But something about his story bothers me."

"What?"

"He's doing something seedy. I can feel it. And to me, that place is still Mom Jon's. I'm going to find out exactly what he's up to, and if he took advantage of her, that shawarma will be the least of his problems."

We went to the first pool, and it was empty. Kids had painted the pool with tags and new-school bullshit. I hated how they gave every picture googly eyes. Everywhere I looked these days, googly eyes on graffiti. There seemed to be no image impervious to fucking googly eyes.

"Should we swim?" Cassidy said, taking the steps down into the graffiti water.

I followed her. "Hope there are no sharks in here."

"A big guy like you? Afraid of some little sharks?" She weaved around the empty pool, wiggling like a fish. "Okay, I checked," she said. "No sharks."

She went to the deep end.

There were a couple of tubes positioned above us that must have plopped people in the pool when the water ran, when this was a place that couldn't possibly kill children.

I joined her down in the deep end.

We stood on a humungous spray-painted picture of an anatomical human heart, with clockwork and gears connecting its chambers.

"Why didn't anyone teach you to drive?" she asked.

"They just didn't."

"They should have."

"But then you couldn't," I said.

She smiled at me, and this one looked way different from the one she'd flashed when we first saw each other through the lobby's glass door. That one was for her job; this one was mine.

And there was no way to properly explain what her smile meant. I'd gone from a cage to the deep end of the pool, from the wolves' smiles to hers. In Quentin, the wolves smiled only for blood. Smiled because people got hurt or killed. Smiled because of a new hustle, a new angle, a new mule, a new soldier. Or a fresh convict came in with dirty paperwork, a charge that would get him stabbed in a couple weeks, unless the wolves kept him alive, protection or extortion, these wolves living like kings of the commissary. They smiled because of how simple society was in there. You took what you could. You could rob anybody inside so long as you weren't a sneak thief, stealing behind anybody's back, so long as you came straight to their face, said, "I'm taking all your shit, and you can't do nothing about it." Then it was up to them if they were willing to jump off to protect what was theirs. You battled for resources and territory and reach and meat. You ran with a pack, or you tried to do your time quietly. But if you didn't square up when somebody stepped to you, you were gonna be eaten.

So those were the only smiles I'd seen for years, and now I was in the deep end of the pool, and time lost its meter, a drunk drummer sloppy with the tempo of seconds. Slowing. Slowing. This was a time to linger, to smell the flowers. A moment like this didn't need any constructive criticism, didn't need a haircut, a hacksaw, a modern spin, a tummy tuck, a smear campaign, an enema, an online lobotomy.

Which was another way of saying: I had my head in the clouds and my head up my ass.

My head was in two useless places.

I wasn't paying attention to anything except Cassidy and the clockwork heart we stood on.

And because of all the useless places I stashed my head, this was when we were ambushed by the women with machine guns.

THERE WERE TEN of them standing above us on the pool's deck. Three came down the steps and stood in the shallow end. They all pointed machine guns at us, except the one who marched forward, a woman, maybe fifty, wearing speckled silver Docs that shimmered like dragon scales.

"You weren't invited into our home," she said.

"You don't need to worry about us," Cassidy said. "I know he looks scary, and sure, he's only a couple days out of prison, but he's a gentle guy. He doesn't even know how to drive."

"You don't need to tell them that," I said.

"You weren't invited into our home," the woman in the silver Docs said again.

It wasn't surprising to find Mom Jon out here with survivalists. Their off-the-grid living situation sounded odd to most, but for Mom Jon, this kind of community made perfect sense. Even in the Haight, Mom Jon and her people would talk about subcultures, free cities built in the carcasses of old industry. They'd talk about it for hours, years, talk about it so often that the words hovered in our house like smog: America was terminally ill with a tumor made of money, and when death rattle capitalism finally gave out, people would need to take care of themselves, and society had made us all so soft that most would break in days. Those who didn't have their minds cracked, a lot of them would starve or die of thirst or be killed fighting for gasoline. Or the threat of those endings would incite such trapped desperation that these people would be led to moral compromises that syphoned the human out of you. That sort of barbarism was usually reserved for men and women in prison, but Mom Jon and company believed it was only a matter of time until it spilled into the streets. They weren't going to let the world's obvious collapse surprise them. Because I knew that about Mom Jon already, I was anxious to see what they'd built here, what little city they'd carved out in this thicket of dinosaur skeletons.

"I'm looking for Mom Jon," I said.

"Never heard of her," the leader said.

"She's family," I said.

"Never heard of her."

"This was her last address."

"Never heard of her," she repeated, which seemed to be a big part of her communication strategy: find a key phrase and fuck it all night.

"She used to live with my aunt, Rebecca, in the Lower Haight," I said. "Once my aunt died, Mom Jon tried to take care of me—before I got locked up . . ."

"You're James?" the woman with the glimmering Docs said, and I nodded at her, and she nodded to her people. The women lowered their machine guns, which was a relief, though I never felt they intended to kill us. They were just protecting what was theirs, and I respected them for that. We shouldn't get mad when people do the right thing, even if it means pointing machine guns at us.

"Is she here?" I asked.

"She's gone."

"Is she coming back?"

"She can't come back," she said, pointing to her brain. "She's gone in here."

The leader told us her name, Val, and led us out of the deep end, up the empty pool's steps, and then we moved deeper into the water park, walking on the craggy patio, drains pocking it like blowholes. All the reclining deck chairs had most of their straps stretched or snapped, so they looked like big, broken instruments.

There was an office building near the center. This had been where security, medical staff, and lifeguards called home while working their shifts. Now, according to Val, it was their headquarters.

In the grassy area next to it, they'd planted crops: broccoli, corn, carrots, avocados, grapes, brussels sprouts. The corn was in two even rows that looked like an equal sign. The fruit on the four avocado trees was young, green, and dimpled. The grapevines grew on and wound around an old lifeguard tower. The carrots, broccoli, and brussels sprouts dawdled dirt-level, slouched like street punks on the sidewalk.

Val led us into headquarters. The lights were all on, fluorescent and too bright and awful, like a grocery store at midnight. They had turned the offices into bunk rooms, and she led us to Mom Jon's.

"We don't know if she's coming back," said Val, "so we're just leaving it like this for now."

Some of her clothes hung on a doorknob. A painting that one of her friends did of our Haight Street house was on the wall. Some books on the floor next to the bed. I didn't even need to look to know they were all poetry. The Beats. They were all she read.

"How long has she been gone?" I asked Val.

"A few months."

I got down onto my knees, looked under the bed for my guitar, but there was nothing there. "You said something's up with her brain. Did she see a doctor?"

"She said that it was vanity to try and cure the body—that we are animals and should die of natural causes. And then her boyfriend took her."

Suddenly, the fluorescent lights felt like flames, like I was a vampire who'd stumbled into the sun. "Took her?" I asked.

"Yes."

"Her boyfriend?"

"Yes."

"Against her will?"

"Yes."

"And she's been with him the last few months?"

"Yes."

"What do you mean when you say he took her against her will?" I asked.

This was what she told me: Jacques was a relatively new addition to their community, in the last year or so, and he and Mom Jon started dating soon after. Even at first, they got into it, both battle dogs, always fighting and making up and fighting, and it got worse between them, these nightly scraps, as her brain melted like an ice cap. His pill business was something their community had recently found out about and wanted no part of, a topic of conversation that Jacques wasn't willing to entertain, and it was put to a vote and decided that he could no longer live among them. He was furious and embarrassed, and he loved Mom Jon, even as they screamed at each other, even as they called each other names and drew blood, and so he told the community to get fucked, he didn't wanna live here anyway. He threw his things into a suitcase, and then he remembered that he was the one who'd planted the corn, so he should at least be corn-compensated for his sweat equity. This was something he knew to be true and fair, and he proclaimed, "I'm taking some fucking corn, thank you very much!" and hauled ass out to the garden, picked as many ears of corn as he could fit into the overstuffed suitcase, and yet he still found this to be an insufficient quantity, so he filled his jeans' front and back pockets with corn, tucked his t-shirt in and fed ears through the neckhole, like storing them in a net, looking thirty months pregnant with corn, and when he finally achieved the necessary load, Jacques waddled back inside their dorms and he called to Mom Jon, "We're leaving," and she said, "I'm not going anywhere," and he said, "We're leaving right now," and she said, "No," and he knocked her down, and he had his suitcase in one hand, and in the other, he had Mom Jon by the hair and dragged her out, Mom Jon, my found family, and she was yelling in agony as he took her against her will, pulled her by the hair from her home, yanked her across the patio, by all the empty pools, past the turnstiles and front gates and through the parking lot, and he tossed her in the passenger side and slid the suitcase in the trunk and shook out all the corn from his person and stored that in the back, too, and he had dragged Mom Jon all the way to his fucking car by the hair, and something was wrong with her brain, and I had to help her.

"Where can I find him?"

"He runs a skydiving school."

"Then," I said, "it's time for me to jump from a plane."

M

On our way out, I needed to follow through on my promise to Cassidy: I told her that I was taking her on a date to a probably haunted water park, so before we continued our quest, we needed to pay our respects to the dead: those waterlogged teenage ghosts.

(Needless to say, Quentin was haunted. How could it not be, that slaughterhouse, that cemetery? We lost so much of ourselves inside. At night, when men sobbed or beat their bare chests, it was impossible to tell the sounds of the living from the dead.)

We climbed the stairs to the top on that sunny afternoon, stood on the lip of the waterslide—*the* waterslide—the one where they all died, and inside the mouth of the slide it was dark, exposing a somehow still humid esophagus, guttural with how the wind whipped through it.

Music.

The blues.

Something down-home.

Something muddy.

From the bayous of Valhalla.

And now, it was time for us to crawl into the dark throat.

First, a question of etiquette. "Would you like to lead the way?" I asked her.

"Hell no. If anyone is accidentally going to fall through the big hole down there, it should be you. Chivalry and shit."

It was a tube slide, so we were completely enclosed, and I had to hunch way down, my height an issue ducking in. It smelled of mildew. There was this curious sense of walking into the past, into an artifact of horror, the worst day of families' lives.

We were only about fifteen feet in, the slide still relatively horizontal before the first big plunge, when we heard a wall of noise inching toward us. Not heard, exactly. Felt. No, that wasn't right, either. We *experienced* a sensation of colliding with a presence, some low static, a rumble.

"Do you . . . is that . . . ?" But Cassidy didn't know how to let herself say it out loud.

So then I tried: "I think it is, Cassidy. I think it's . . . them."

We crouched in the dark throat, my body so hunched over that my thighs and lower back burned, as their gruff roars washed upon us, birthed by a haunted organ. They were space aliens, swan maidens, mariachi bands, demolition derbies, satellite dishes, champagne toasts. They were angels who rented their wings as billboards. They were asthma inhalers, an EpiPen loaded with a mother's love, a Bible with every other page missing. They were squandered stardust, and Cassidy and I had been hand selected by Odin to hear this song.

"Are they pissed?" Cassidy asked me. "I can't tell if they sound pissed or not."

"They are definitely pissed," I said. "What we don't know is if they're mad at us."

The ghost kids kept cussing, hissing, livid about their luck and gone futures. Cassidy reached her hand out to mine in the dim, ethereal light of the tube, in the throat of their church, as the kids doused us in their melancholy.

"I have to hand it to you," she whispered. "You promised a probably haunted water park, and here we are."

"I wasn't lying."

"I don't want to go any farther," she said.

"No, we aren't invited," I said, then cupped my hands over my mouth and spoke directly to the kids: "We won't bother you again!"

Their voices gushed, crescendoed, rang up from the guts, a chain saw, a volcano. This was their sacred place, and we weren't welcome, which was fine by me: Not all cemeteries want visitors.

Before we turned to leave, we indulged in another few seconds of their breath and got high on a stretch of eye contact with each other, indulged in the commotion of new feelings and a new adventure that led us into an unmarked cemetery dangling in the sky.

"I'm having a lot of fun," Cassidy said. "Are you?"

"I'm having the time of my life."

A couple minutes later, right as we emerged from the slide's mouth at its top, Cassidy asked, "Can I do something dumb?"

"Sure. Wait. What kind of dumb?"

"I want to tell them something."

I pointed down the throat. "*Them* them?"

"Yeah."

"Should I leave so you have privacy?"

"No," she said, "I need you to hear it, too. It's about my brother. He's dead. He's why I need that hundred grand from Tony." Then she shouted to the ghosts, "He was young! Like you!"

The teenage ghosts growled.

Cassidy's body changed its hum. She got slow in her movements and breathing, and it almost seemed like she'd left herself, left here—went there, meaning the past. She had that haunted frequency, anxious, frantic, and those kinds of memories were tar pits.

Then in a kind of trance, Cassidy spoke to the teenage ghosts and me: "He got a brain tumor. Cedric. That's his name. The last time I went to see him, he asked me to bring him a bag of oranges. Twelve years between us, so I was more an auntie than a sister. I was the oldest;

he, the youngest. And we'd chomp on oranges by the bagful growing up. Poor as fuck and oranges were a meal and dessert and the next meal. I resented oranges. Don't even like 'em, really. But I did with him. Our mom was long gone at this point. She had six kids with five different men. That last time, I called Cedric's dad and told him that I was coming to say goodbye to Ced. That was when my brother requested I bring a bag of oranges, ripe and ready to go. Like old times, he said. I spent all afternoon sitting next to his hospital bed with the bag of fruit, but he said he wasn't hungry. I didn't push. I didn't know."

She was in it now. The tar rose and poured freely into her mouth. Maybe it tasted like orange juice.

"The crazy thing was," she said, "I sat next to his hospital bed all day, into the evening, and we didn't eat one orange. We listened to Nina Simone. We told old stories. The bag of oranges sat there, untouched. He said he hadn't been hungry in weeks. Eventually, I left. Then a few days later, Ced died. Right in that hospital bed at home. When his daddy called to tell me, I went over to the house to help with his stuff, and the bag of oranges was still right next to the bed—but because they'd been in that stuffy house, they'd all turned moldy. Decomposed. The whole bag of them. These fuzzy blue balls. I was thinking about those whiskers on the fruit, and I told his dad that I'd like to scatter Ced's ashes in a grove not far from the house. My brother would've liked that. I know it in my bones. I expected his father to agree, yes, that was a perfect resting place, but instead, he said that he'd let me have the ashes only if I bought them from him. Fucker was gonna try to make money off his son's death. Can you believe that? I didn't know what to do. I was heartbroken, holding a bag of moldy oranges. My first thought was to heave the dusty fruit at him, like beaning a batter with a baseball. But the dumb oranges were all I had left of him. And then Ced's father said something so horrible that I'll think about it till my dying day."

She shouted to the ghosts down the dark throat: "Are you ready to hear my secret?"

Their rumbles rose. The tar was up to her hair now. I'd never heard somebody talk while submerged, but she was swimming in the memory. She lived there now.

"Ready to hear my secret, too?" she asked me.

There was nothing in the world I wanted more. She'd destroyed me by saying that somebody had the gall to hold ashes for ransom. That was a fact so grim it tattooed to my brain, and I could think of nothing else. We were so weak. Our bodies were plastic bags of molecules. That was all we were made of—and because of that, I needed to hear her secret.

Cassidy said, "His bastard dad told me that the only reason Ced didn't want to eat the oranges with me that day was because he was embarrassed. Cedric was too weak, couldn't peel them. He didn't want to tell me. My own baby brother, so feeble that he couldn't peel an orange—one orange!—and I was too stupid to see it and help him. I'm so mad at myself and I'm so mad at his pride. It would have been my honor to peel him one more." Then she softened, looked right at me: "Why didn't it dawn on me? Why couldn't I see it? Why didn't I help him eat one last orange before he died?"

She asked the same question three different ways and then began to cry. The growls from the tube grew ambient, a humming.

"I can't remember," she said, "being that disappointed in myself. That was when I named his father Daddy Nightmares. He broke my heart, broke me. I stood there clutching that bag of blue-and-green oranges. They smelled earthy, eerie. I bolted ass out of the house with the fruit, and I knew what I had to do, and I knew it would tear me to pieces, knew I'd puke and shit and maybe end up in the emergency room or a coffin, and none of it mattered. I knew all that, but I didn't care. Not one single hair on my body cared. I did it for him. I did it because I could. I did it because I had strong fingers. I did it because I should have done it for Ced. I peeled every single one of our fucking oranges. And I ate all the dead fruits."

OUT IN THE PARKING LOT of Slide City, I was behind the wheel of a 1980s Corvette.

Cassidy, California sober, was in the passenger seat, smoking a joint, using it to indicate certain features around the car as she gave me the bare essentials. Currently, she pointed the joint down at the pedals. "That foot's the brake. That's the gas. Here are all the gears, but really, it's only P, R, and D you need to know. What's neutral? Beats me. Then a couple just have numbers, while all the rest are letters? Ignore the numbers. That's my advice. I've never used them and I'm a great driver. And you're already holding the wheel, so not much to say there. You have mirrors. I don't use them. Use your eyes. Your eyes are better than mirrors. And that's all you need to know about driving."

She took a huge pull of the joint and blew the smoke out the window.

I was still thinking about what she'd said about her brother's ashes being held for a hundred-thousand-dollar ransom. I didn't know how to let that go.

"What are you waiting for?" she said after a few seconds.

I put the Corvette in gear, tapped the accelerator, and cranked the machine up to a solid fifteen miles an hour, and we puttered around.

"What the hell are you doing?" she said.

"I'm warming up."

"This is embarrassing."

"I'll be ready for twenty miles an hour soon."

"A death-defying achievement."

"I made a reservation at his skydiving school. I'm going up tomorrow. Do you want to come along?"

"I thought you just needed to find him."

"I do."

"So why do you need to skydive?"

"Because I was in San Quentin a few days ago," I said, "and I want to be in the sky."

"Yeah, well, you should stop driving like a pussy first," she said, and I cranked the Corvette up to a cool thirty. We did laps in the abandoned parking lot.

"I'm going to hurt this man," I said to her.

"I know."

"He deserves it."

"I'm not gonna tell you to be careful, because fuck careful. I hate careful. But I like you," she said, "so maybe you could be just a little careful. A touch careful."

"I'm only driving fifty miles an hour," I said, circling on our deserted NASCAR track.

Cassidy threw the inch of joint out the window, and it fluttered in the wind like a moth.

"The day we met was rough for me," she said. "Selling real estate is awful. It's what you do if you're not flexible enough to be a yoga instructor. These are bimbo jobs, and I'm a woman so I can say that. And selling real estate without eyebrows? I wanted to die. I couldn't even imagine being the real estate lady. A life sentence of always talking square footage and floor plans and somebody putting a gun in my mouth. Then you walked in."

I stopped the car.

"What are you doing?" she asked.

I slid the Corvette into reverse and drove backward now, craning around to use my good eye to see where we were going. "I don't trust mirrors, too."

"Good boy," she said. "And you're gonna be a touch careful, right?"

I didn't want to lie to her, and I also didn't want to tell the truth. I didn't want her to hear that the malice of this world made me do crazy, joyous things. My problem was that I wanted to live like a monkey who'd never seen the sky.

I tried a joke instead, hoping she wouldn't notice, and either it worked or she let me wriggle from the hook. "You don't need to sell real estate," I said to her. "You can open a driving school. You can use me as your first testimonial. I came to you with no vehicular talent to speak of, and look at me now: I can go backward!"

That made Cassidy laugh.

"I can't take all the credit," she said. "You have some natural ability."

I **WAS ELBOWS-DEEP** in a trough of the Almighty again. My mohawk was stuffed in a hairnet. I was rubbing egg and breadcrumbs and herbs into the meat. Python Wally kneaded his dune, too.

"Meatloaf again?" I said to him.

"You'll find this is a staple of our diet around here."

"How much of a staple are we talking?"

"Every day, basically."

"The poor plumbing."

"Our bodies' or the building's?" Python asked, then he startled, said, "Shit, my nose." He took one of his gloves off, rubbed like crazy. "I think something bit me."

"Like a bee?"

"I don't know."

"Are there bedbugs here?" I asked.

"Keep the bedbugs out of the meatloaf," he said. "Sounds like a blues song," and he started to sing, *Keep the bedbugs out of the meatloaf*, and I joined him, the two of us wailing the line over and over, Wally re-gloving his hand and the two of us working our meat troughs and giving this song everything we had.

As we wrapped it up, Python asked, "So what are you going to do so you don't go back?"

I knew I was messing up, but how could I not help Cassidy? How did you walk away from somebody who'd had her eyebrows shaved? Now there was Mom Jon, Tony, the scam, Jacques, the missing happy monster. These all seemed like topics best omitted during this meatloaf heart-to-heart with Python.

"I don't know yet," I said.

"You need to be working toward something," said Wally. "Purpose. That's what we need out here. You're fucked without purpose." I must've flashed a face baked in ire, because he immediately asked me, "Are you mad at me, or mad at the truth?"

Nobody had ever posed such a question to me before, and it was simple and pure and marvelous: How many times during our lives did we resent people because it was easier than staring the truth dead in the eyes?

Our four paws formed the meat into mounds, rectangles, swelling into railroad ties. We were building food with our bare hands, and we were talking about building a life, and it all should have made so much sense to me, should have made the life outside of Quentin shine like a diamond, and maybe it did. Maybe I was under the spell of a different diamond, a bigger one, a jewel that gleamed with danger.

"I want to work toward joy," I said to him.

"Joy? You might be the first convict here to ever use that word. I bet there are some here who don't even know what it means."

"I know I'm supposed to want peace," I said, "but I don't know how."

"Every man bunking here has that gene."

"What gene?"

"The one that whispers, *Hey, should we ruin our life right now?*"

"I just lost eight years of my life," I said, "so I'm not doing one more goddamn thing that doesn't bring me joy."

"You're not thinking about it right," said Wally. "You shouldn't do one more goddamn thing that doesn't keep you on the outside. That's where joy is. On the outside."

I knew what he meant—there was joy outside of prison, not in it—and he was right about that. But I meant joy inside the body, meant joy that felt like adrenaline, a drug, an orgasm.

Python Wally was right about purpose, which was another reason I wanted my happy monster back.

"Music," I said. "That's my purpose."

"That's a hobby," he said.

"A passion."

"A passionate, purposeful hobby," he said.

"I'm starting to hate you," I said.

"Hate me all you want," he said, "but purpose is the only thing that will keep you from going back to the slaughterhouse."

For a minute, we were quiet, and all you could hear was the squish of meat in our wringing hands.

"Well," he finally said, "you and your joy and your unemployed purpose can crash on my couch."

"I can be a real musician. My old man made art. If he could do it, so can I. He even—"

"Jesus, please don't start talking about your childhood," said Wally.

"I'm saying he made a living making art. Why can't I?"

"You have the look," Python said, "of someone fucking up."

"What is the look, exactly?"

"It's the one right before you get busted back."

I started to pack some of the Almighty into a Quonset hut-style shape on my baking pan.

"Why do you want to go back?" Python asked. He took his hands out of the meat and held them up, pieces of flesh like pink ants pilled on his hands. "What's your hurry to go back to that hell? All we want to do is leave there, so why do so many of us sprint back? Why can't we fucking learn to take care of ourselves?"

"I'm trying to find somebody I love," I said, and put my arms through the Quonset hut, pulling the pink temple down. "I owe her that. She gave me a home once. I need to know that she's okay."

"I hope you find her," he said, "and I hope you don't go back." He plunged his hands in deep and made fists in the meat, a noise that sounded like the whimpers of baby birds. "The problem is you want to live like you're prime rib, but people like us, we're meatloaf."

ᛗ

On the plane, it was me, Jacques, and a pilot who wore his pilot cap backward, which sort of bothered me. One detail I did like: punk rock played. Jacques had asked me if I liked music right before takeoff, said we could listen to whatever I wanted, and since we were headed into the heavens, I felt like listening to Joe Strummer.

Right now, Joe screamed that we needed to know our rights.

This was long after I'd paid Jacques almost a thousand dollars from my Tony advance on a last-minute private lesson, and because he wanted the money, he didn't ask any questions. Here was how our tandem dive was supposed to work: our bodies strapped together—me in front of him—so that he, as the experienced diver, could navigate our descent and landing.

Jacques and I wore blue jumpsuits. We had goggles on our foreheads, had our harnesses on; they were connected to seat belts mounted to the walls to hold us in during takeoff and for the climb. We weren't tethered together yet. No, that was gonna happen at about fifteen hundred feet, he told me, getting tandemed up, tightening our straps, leaping out when we reached the exit altitude of about ten thousand.

I had a head full of hot ideas.

Joe Strummer sang, *You agree to be investigated, humiliated . . .*

And that was how I knew it was time.

Me unbuckling my seat belt.

"Hey," Jacques said, "you can't do that."

Me standing up.

"Sit down," he said.

"You're about to have a very bad day," I said to him, "but first, let's jump out of a plane."

"Sit the fuck down!"

"I just got out of Quentin. Can you imagine that, Jacques? Going from being locked up to flying?"

On the plane's wall, a light came on that indicated it was go time. I clipped us together, even though he tried to fight me on it. I had a hundred pounds on him, and there was nothing he could do, and with a couple quick steps, I powered us from the plane.

It was like being on a motorcycle that had a cocaine habit; it was a surfboard gliding on the side of a frozen skyscraper; it was a syringe loaded with agitated cheetahs—

We were happy monsters.

Or I was.

I should only speak for myself.

I got the feeling that Jacques wasn't having as much fun as me, but I wouldn't let his little tantrum sully this.

No, this was my sky,
my speed,
my wind,
my clouds,
my air,
my birds,
my bugs—
this was my pollution,
and I couldn't even remember what it was like to be in a cage,
no, that was another life,
this was two men free-falling,
a smile on my face,
a freeze in my ears,
falling with my eye closed,
have you ever tried it?
I was being far out,
I laughed like the first fish to ooze out of the ocean and
draw a breath into land-lungs and
fall in love and
hail a taxi and
crash a funeral to dance with the dead.
I screamed myself hoarse,
berserker happy,
tied to a total stranger,
a lazy quesadilla,
a Chairman Mao,
a blacksmith,

a yellowjacket,

a vagina monologue,

a sophisticated rabbi.

I wanted to tattoo a sonnet on my tongue so every time I talked it sounded like poetry.

I wanted to paint a self-portrait and sign it in lightning.

Then Jacques opened our parachute.

Slowing us fast, sure, but not sobering me up, hell no, still liquored on sky. Looking out at the smoggy horizon of this dumb world that I didn't know how to stop loving.

I would have my feet back on the ground soon.

WE LANDED IN A DIRT FIELD, surrounded by almond trees. A van waited nearby to pick us up, one that was piloted by a guy wearing camo overalls. I unhitched myself from Jacques, climbed from the parachute, and sped over to the van. The driver's-side window was down, so I leaned close and said, "Give me the fucking keys, or I'll hit you so hard you forget your ATM pin."

He agreeably coughed them up.

"Give me your phone, too," I said.

"Oh no, it's pretty new," he said.

"I'm not stealing it. I'll leave it back at your office."

Once he handed it over, I left him sitting behind the wheel, watching while I went back over to Jacques, yanking him to his feet. I slid behind him, my chest to his back, and put him in a rear naked choke.

He was barely conscious. I loosened my grip some, but I kept it uncomfortable for him.

It was time for a blood choke chat.

"Your friend's watching from the van," I said to Jacques, then I yelled to the guy in the van, "Wave!" and he put a paw out the window in reluctant compliance.

Jacques tried to wave back, but it was complicated with me squeezing his neck.

"Where is Mom Jon?" I asked Jacques.

"Our new house," he wheezed.

"She's sick?"

"Yeah."

"What does she have?"

"She won't go to the doctor."

"Her brain?"

"Can't remember nothing."

"Val told me you push pills. Is Mom Jon on your shit??"

"What pills?"

I pulled my shoulders back, tightening the choke.

"We party, yeah," he whispered.

"I heard a story about you," I said, "one about dragging her around by her hair," and I snatched two handfuls of his hair, using my grip to steer his head. He scampered, trying to keep up with the speed of his traveling hair in my mitts, but he fell behind, and I could feel the follicles loosen some. I wasn't going to pull out his hair. I was going to do something way worse to him than that, but for now, I wanted him to think that I was about to scalp him.

"Why did you put your hands on her?" I said.

"I try not to."

"You try not to?"

"It's hard."

"Those weren't the right answers," I said, and then I stopped dragging him and grabbed his wrist and swung his forearm toward my knee, breaking his bone.

He fell down into the white parachute, which looked like the petal of a prehistoric flower. And it looked so beautiful to me, made me forget to breathe. Life could just crack your head in half. I could hear bagpipes, extraterrestrials, hear the ancestors howl, hear dolphins plotting to overthrow the government. I eavesdropped on a lonely matador throwing his cape down and asking the bull if he would rather tango.

"I love Mom Jon," I said to Jacques.

"So do I!" he said, down on the flower petal, shrieking in pain.

"Should I keep breaking limbs?"

"I'm probably in shock." He put his hands to his head, wincing at the broken arm. "Shock, yeah," he said. "This is for sure shock."

"What's your address?" I said.

"I can't remember. My head's too loopy."

"Sure, you can."

"I can't find my address in my head. They're showing cartoons in there."

"Then I'll break your other arm."

"We live in the Merry Days," he said. "It's a development out in the desert."

"The Merry Days?" I frog-marched Jacques to the van, threw him in the passenger seat. I walked around and ushered the man in overalls out of the vehicle, and I hopped in.

"Why can't I just get a ride with you guys?" Sergeant Overalls wondered.

"Your boss slings pills," I said to him, "so you can't go to the cops. You can walk your ass back and forget we met."

"Hey, man, if you say I'm walking, I'm walking," he said. "I want to remember my ATM pin. That's my priority here."

Jacques and I peeled back toward the street. He didn't know it yet, but we were on our way to burn his plane.

M

Cassidy was waiting for us back at Jacques's office and hangar. She'd give us a ride back to SF so we could dump Jacques off at Tony's until tomorrow, when we'd go to the Merry Days for Mom Jon. There wasn't enough time before curfew at the halfway house today.

This stretch of the small airport was run-down, remote. We were the only people around. Two of the neighboring hangars had their doors open with nothing inside, and by that I didn't just mean empty of planes but literally nothing.

I brought him up to speed on what I expected from him as we carpooled in the van: When we arrived, he was to immediately send his assistant, the pilot, and the mechanic home. And I had to give him credit, he gave the performance of his career, really selling these commands. Before we knew it, everyone had left for the day.

Cassidy was in the waiting room reading a magazine. I asked for a few minutes alone with him, and she agreed, provided I exercised a touch or two of careful. "Don't cut anything off him," she said.

"Wait, what?" Jacques said.

Now, it was just the two of us, Jacques and me, in the hangar, about to have a heart-to-heart.

"Sit down," I said to Jacques, and he followed the instruction, plopping in a chair.

"Cover your eyes," I said, and he placed his palms over them.

"Now don't you move a muscle," I said, and he turned into a mannequin.

I stood in front of him, wishing this were the Old World and I could simply split his skull and return to my home, play with my children, gather around the table for a home-cooked meal. There shouldn't be consequences for killing a coward. But I was doing my best not to murder him, and so I arrived at the solution of lighting his plane on fire. If what Val had said to me was true—that he used the skydiving school as a cover to push product—his suppliers and pill partners would be furious if his plane was out of commission. I'd let them sort him out.

I nabbed a coiled hose from a nail on the hangar's wall, along with a bucket, and I began the process of siphoning the gas from the plane, giving my side of the hose a grand suck, and here came the flow.

Once it was emptying into the bucket, I said to Jacques, "The world has too many people like you."

"You don't even know me," he said.

"I know that I've decided to change your life," I said, and the gas tank was sucked dry, and the bucket was half full, not half empty, because it was hard not to be an optimist after recently falling from the sky.

"Change it how?" he asked.

I moved to the wall where several pairs of coveralls hung on hooks, and I threw them all over my shoulder and trudged the laundry to the plane, threw all the clothes inside, splashed some gas from the bucket on them.

Jacques, eyes still covered, still remaining perfect still, said, "I smell fuel."

I lit a match, and the kindling of clothing went up in flames inside the plane.

He sniffed the air, like an animal sensing danger on the horizon. "Is something on fire now?"

"Yeah."

"Are you going to kill me?"

"No."

"Will you tell me what's on fire?"

"I'll let you answer that question for yourself," I said.

"Does that mean I can look?"

"You can look."

"So you're giving me permission to move?"

"Yes, move."

He uncovered his eyes, blinked, gasped.

For a minute, he studied the burning plane.

"That's my plane, and it's on fire," he said.

I'd seen many men in Quentin suffer gruesome injuries, seen an army of them stabbed or bludgeoned or choked to death in front of me. Even when I knew they earned these crime scenes, it always made me feel bad watching the violence between these bored Vikings. They had nothing to do in there all day but kill one another, so that was what they did. Because I'd witnessed so much of that waste, I thought I might even feel a tad bad for Jacques, setting the inside of his plane on fire.

Nope. Not at all.

This felt like a trophy, a hit record, a gold-plated blow job.

We watched the plane blaze. The windows cracked, popped. The cockpit wobbled with reds, yellows, oranges. The dune of coveralls burned to charred snowflakes, blowing around the hangar with the weather and energy from the fire.

"And why did you do that to my plane?" he asked.

"Because if you ever touch her again, I'll dump your dead body in the ocean."

We fell quiet while the fire ate everything it could inside the plane, before slowly beginning to go out in the metal husk. Cassidy came into the hangar and said, "This doesn't seem a touch careful. Do you know what it means? *Careful*? Should we look *careful* up in the fucking dictionary together?"

ᛗ

We loaded Jacques in the trunk and tore ass toward SF, back to Tony's office. I knew every minute, once I was back at the halfway house for the night, would tease me—*Ha ha, you're so close and so far away*—and time was a gateway drug to despair. To say I was distracted and surly would be to trample on the good names of distracted and surly, those twins, those fuses.

So Cassidy drove us—me, distracted and surly—to my temporary employer, and Jacques made punk rock from the trunk. In another life, he could have been up onstage at Gilman threatening all us punks with his lyrics. All the shock from first seeing his plane on fire had subsided, and now he raged like a god hopped up on spite. "Oh, sure, burn another man's plane!" he said from the trunk. "That's what you do, huh?! That's your signature fucking move?! You wake up and say, *Hey, whose fucking plane can I burn today?! Whose life can I ruin?* Well, I won't forget this! I'll get even! I have to! Because you're not only a plane burner, you're an arm maimer! And I'll get even somehow!"

One might think that was enough yelling in one car at one time. Yes, one might think that the yelling fella in the trunk was about the proper amount of hollering.

But in addition to Jacques's noise, Cassidy was more upset than I'd seen her. She was a grenade wearing perfume. "And you listen to me?" she said to me. "This is something you need to hear!"

"I am trying my best to listen," I said, "but he's really going back there."

"Shut the fuck up!" Cassidy said to Jacques.

A suggestion he did not take.

So she screamed to him, "Don't make me do the exhaust-pipe-hose thing and gas you! I don't want to! But I will!! I'll do the exhaust-pipe-hose thing!"

This suggestion was met with prompt compliance.

Quiet. The way a trunk should sound.

We passed a cluster of semis lined up on the shoulder, all shuddering, like withdrawing rhinos.

All the yelling they were doing, and all the screaming in my brain about not making it to the Merry Days today, squeezed my organs, compressed all these stampeding feelings to a ninety-second song of ire. I said to Cassidy, "Please stop yelling."

"That wasn't a touch careful," she said, speaking back at a normal volume. "I don't like careful any better than you do, but just a touch wasn't going to kill you."

"You're right."

"I like you," she said, "and I don't want you to go back."

Suddenly, those peaks of distracted and surly lost their altitude, plummeted to sea level. Cassidy cared about me. She found a way to care about someone as discardable as me.

"I don't want that, either," I said.

"Then stop burning people's planes," she said.

"Yeah!" Jacques said from the trunk.

How crazy was our world? This was a place where you could find joy while somebody yelled in the trunk.

"You want the gas?!" she said to him.

"No thanks!" he said.

"I'll stop burning planes," I said to her, and I meant it; I wanted to learn how to live like that. But what made such a flagrant impression on me right then wasn't what I felt but what her words made clear about Cassidy, and how long had it been since somebody was concerned about me? Between her and Python basically saying the same thing, maybe I should learn how to heed and listen.

I sat next to Cassidy in the Corvette, and we were speeding, and the Cramps were singing again, and I smiled.

Cassidy softened. "Sorry for screaming," she said. "Sometimes I get the crazies."

"I get the crazies, too."

"Yeah, no shit."

"I'm working on it."

"Still a ways to go," she said.

This seemed like a rip-the-Band-Aid type of moment, so I said to her, "Speaking of that, my crazies want to do something illegal for you."

"We are literally talking about you being more careful right this very second," she said.

"I want to get your brother's ashes," I said.

Her face turned sultry, sexy, and she said, "That's the most romantic thing anyone's ever said to me. Do you think I can keep the Corvette at seventy and kiss you at the same time?"

And that was exactly what we did.

Everybody alive, we were all these tire fires, these mangled muscle cars. We had that startling dissonance of thinking we mattered in a world that knew we didn't. Our lives collided randomly with one another. Cassidy could have refused the eyebrow bet and not been the realtor that day. Or I could've gone to Mom Jon's on a different morning. Or I could've been released late, early, stabbed on my way out the door. But we met and now we were kissing in a Corvette at seventy miles an hour.

Then I did one of the dumbest things we could do as humans: I assumed the best about the future.

WE TIED JACQUES UP next to Tony at the office. They sat near the back of the room, by the desk. Everybody needed companionship in this life.

"Who's this?" Tony asked me.

"That's Jacques," I said. "Like you, he is also on my shit list."

"He burned my plane," said Jacques to Tony. "He broke my arm."

"He stood by and witnessed an act of fecal assault on my fish tank," Tony said, as an apparent counter.

"It doesn't surprise me to hear that," Jacques said. "Sounds like the exact behavior of a plane-burning asshole."

"Feel free to duct-tape Jacques's mouth," I said to Cassidy, a suggestion that she decided to act on. In ten seconds, his maw was covered, and he stared at us murderously.

"Why no tape for Tony?" she asked me.

"Because he's going to start talking," I said, "or I'm going to start hurting him."

This was an empty threat. I had no plans to actively hurt Tony because I knew he'd cave. The question was: How many days would he need to spend tied to the chair?

"Before I start torturing you," I said to him, "I'm gonna head over to your aquarium and see what that forty grand's worth of fish is actually worth."

I had an ex-girlfriend who had a big saltwater aquarium that she never kept clean, algae spackling the walls in patterns that looked like jungle camouflage. Your only hope to see inside was to cup your hands around your eyes and bring your face up to the glass. Even then, you couldn't see the fish directly, only watch their blurry bodies pass in streaks of muddled colors.

Tony's tank was tended with far more TLC than hers. Or it had been until Cassidy decided to use it as a toilet. Her hypothesis had been right: All the fish were fine in there, though the water was murky, the tank's light casting scrawny rays.

Because of my ex, I knew that Tony would have to have a bucket and a tube to siphon out water so he could regularly change it, though in her case these supplies went mostly unused.

"You leave my fish alone!" Tony said.

"It's not the fishes' fault," Cassidy said to me, then: "I can't believe I'm defending fish. Or agreeing with Tony."

"Can I talk to you in private?" I asked her, and she followed me into the office's small bathroom, and I told her the plan. I had ninety minutes before curfew at the halfway house, so I needed to hustle and hop on BART soon. Cassidy couldn't drive me to the East Bay because we needed her here, guarding them. It didn't feel right, leaving her with the night shift, but I didn't have a choice. Plus, after I'd assured the fishes' safety, she said the night shift was no sweat by saying, "I'm a modern woman who carries a gun."

I wasn't going to let Jacques go free until I saw Mom Jon, where she lived, how she lived, what kind of care she received. He'd lost a plane today, but if I didn't like whatever we walked into with Mom Jon, he was going to have an even worse day tomorrow.

Cassidy and I reentered the office from the bathroom. Tony and Jacques watched in silence as I walked across the room to the aquarium. There was a cupboard built into its stand, and I assumed the supplies I needed to siphon the water and snag the fish would be there. Those supplies were indeed stashed inside, but as I ducked down to retrieve the bucket, I glimpsed a dull glimmer behind it. Something was mounted on the back wall of the cupboard: rows of keys hanging off hooks. A lot of keys with addresses taped to them. One of them was for Unit 12.

Why would anybody keep keys like that? I pulled all the keys off their hooks and stacked them in an outstretched palm, walked them over and scattered them on Tony's desk.

"That's a strange place to keep keys," I said.

Tony shook his head, so I headed back to the tank, opened its lid; I ran one side of the tube into the water, sucked on the other to start the flow.

"What are you doing?" Tony asked.

"I'm going to flush your fish down the toilet."

"Those fish are my family!" he said, panicking, bucking under his rope, thrashing in his chair.

I liked watching his sad spectacle. It was authentic and desperate, a show of care that felt impossible from an eyebrow thief. It was one of the things I loved most about us, the way we protected what we loved, the way we loved what we protected. Even assholes like Tony loved things.

"If you care about them," I said, "then save their lives."

The bucket was already filled with siphoned water, and I retrieved the small net from the cupboard, began to scoop up the fish, plop them in their temporary home.

"Something tells me those hidden keys," I said, nabbing two fish, "have something to do with what you don't want to tell us."

There were four of his fish in the bucket, and that was enough to launch his torment. I'd use his brain against him. Minds were cause-and-effect machines. Our heads were slaughterhouses and nurseries, insane asylums and courtrooms, concert halls and art museums, carnivals and orgasms, bubble baths and war. And if our heads were so many things at once, what did that say about the peculiar music in our skulls?

"I'm done asking you questions that you won't answer, Tony," I said, carrying the sloshing bucket to the bathroom.

"No!" Tony shouted.

I set the bucket down next to the toilet, but not before splashing some of its contents into the bowl for effect (no fish). Then I flushed the empty toilet.

"That was the one with the orange-and-black body," I called out, peeping the one I described swimming around the bucket in a carefree manner. The creature seemed to know I wasn't that kind of barbarous god; I'd never hurt something that didn't earn it.

"My clown fish," he said. "Her name was Cinnamon."

"Sounds like a stripper," Cassidy said.

"I've had her the longest," Tony moaned.

"You killed her!" I yelled.

I flushed the toilet again.

"That was the blue one!"

"My damsel," he said. "Roo."

I poked my head out from the bathroom so he could see me while tied to his desk chair. Jacques, with the duct tape over his mouth, listened to us with the wide eyes of a child hearing a ghost story.

"The next one looks like a punk rocker," I said. "Its body is striped in earth tones, and it has a big spiked mohawk."

"No!" Tony said. "That's my lionfish, Sheila. You can't kill Sheila!"

"*You* are killing Sheila," I said, "in five seconds."

"Those hidden keys are all their properties!" Tony said.

"*All* the properties?" Cassidy echoed.

"Those are the ones they keep vacant."

"The corporate investor you mentioned," I helped him along.

"Don't hurt Sheila."

"The corporate investor?" I repeated.

"Yes!"

"Why do they keep them vacant?"

"Drives up the cost of their other places when they rent them out or flip them. Less supply, more demand."

You were a person, and I was a person, and we were in a bathroom with a bucket full of fish, and we finally had our first picture of this brand of capitalism, the cruelty. People like me would never get ahead if we played by the rules of a rigged world. We'd keep working blue-collar jobs and paying overpriced rents because other people could afford empty houses and keep them that way, just to squeeze a few more dollars from our overworked souls. Our feet ached from working eight hours hustling around a restaurant. Our elbows and shoulders ached from pounding them at construction sites. We nannied the brats of tech workers and stunk like dirty diapers. We delivered your food on rainy days so you could stiff us on the tip.

"And the point of fake open houses?"

"Optics," Tony said. "The sales need to look legit."

"So you really did just shave my eyebrows to be an asshole," Cassidy said to him.

"I shouldn't have done that," he said.

"Flush Sheila!" Cassidy said to me.

"Sheila! No!" Tony cried.

I flushed the empty toilet.

Suddenly and extravagantly, a plan began its righteous hatching, and all I could do was smile. The plans that came to me were always like this—divine, spontaneous answers to prayers. Every now and again, the serfs had to rise and fight. And as the toilet refilled, my new plan found shape, a body, one bulging with reckless joy, what my people call "wunjo."

The fish were, of course, safe in the bucket, but since Tony couldn't see inside it, I carried the bucket back to the aquarium, pretending it was empty. I started to scoop out more of Tony's fish family.

"What's your arrangement with them?" I asked him.

"I help them buy empty units. That's all I do."

"And shave eyebrows," said Cassidy.

I carried the bucket to Tony, dropped it heavily down at his feet so he could see his family in there, lackadaisical but unharmed in their studio apartment. You should have seen his relief. It reminded me of a bizarre word: *miracle*. I never understood its true meaning. From what I could gather, a miracle was when you got what you wanted but found it essential to assign its reality to someone else's will. Or another way to say it: A miracle was when you believed that we were all secret keys in a god's cupboard.

Anything was a miracle if you misunderstood the noise of a toilet flush.

In the end, it didn't matter, because both of us received our wish: Tony's fish were back from the dead, and I wouldn't have to hurt him.

"My babies are alive in a bucket," Tony said in clear wonderment.

I could relate. Punk rockers lived in buckets. Crappy buckets getting more expensive every day with unruly rents, helped along by these empty units. There was not a fucking chance I was gonna let this slide.

"In total, how many properties do they have in SF?" I said to tied-up Tony, with tied-up-and-gagged Jacques sitting next to him.

"About forty vacants."

"And those are the keys to them all?"

"Yes."

"Then it's settled," I said, and I gazed at Cassidy again. We'd be a touch careful soon—soon!—and I meant that, but right now, no, this was gonna require a certain disposition made of furious Viking thrills. These were the same kicks my ancestors had getting even with an interloping king. There was nothing, not one thing, that made me feel more alive than righteous battle.

"You and I are going on about forty new dates," I said to Cassidy.

She clapped but also had a sheen of concern. "Why? What are we going to do?"

"We're gonna pull the ol' Sid & Nancy," I said.

"What the hell does that mean?" she asked.

And with that, my plan had a name: the Ol' Sid & Nancy.

Yeah, we needed those punk rock spirit animals to guide our mania.

PART 3

THE OL' SID & NANCY

YOU RUSTY CADAVER, you pincushion catharsis, you horny Sasquatch, you obscene mongoose, you smashed Bentley, you bear hug, you fanny pack—

I have bad news.

The Ol' Sid & Nancy would have to wait a day or two. Because tomorrow, first thing, I had to get Mom Jon. And tonight I was at the halfway house, waiting for the writing class, with an unruly anvil of the Almighty throbbing in my gut. I'd faked a migraine to get out of my dinner prep shift with Python Wally earlier. There was no way I could tell him about the airplane.

I was under the BE FAR OUT! The teacher, Harding, walked in wearing another tracksuit, all black this time, with a different pair of Jordans. These sneakers were all black, too. He came right up to me: "You'll hear another graduation story tonight. You need to start thinking about what you want to write about in here."

I didn't have to think about it at all. "I already know."

"You can't already know," he said, "because I haven't told you the one rule yet."

"I'm a punk rocker, and I don't care about rules."

"You'll care about this one, motherfucker," he said to me, "if you want me to help you. And I do. I want to help you write your story."

Harding stared at me, and I stared back. Two elephants measuring our trunks down by the watering hole. But he wanted to help me, to teach me, and I wanted to write a Viking saga, a bloodred quest of tenderness and revenge. You couldn't scribble a legend without an open wound.

Harding didn't have to be here. He was being generous with his time and mind, and I should be appreciative. "Okay," I said, "what's your rule?"

"It is very simple and very hard," he said, "and it's the only way to find truth on the page."

I put my hand out for a proper shake. Harding looked at my hand like it was made of dogshit.

"Learn to dap," he said, and walked to the front of the class.

Suddenly, I felt desperate to hear it: "You didn't tell me what the rule was!"

Harding said, "Write what you know—but never write what you understand."

I didn't understand anything. How did my mother die dancing on a bar? How did my father kill himself in front of me? How did Rebecca get off that bus, leaving me without any family? How did I become a junkie? Why did I become a junkie? Why did I slam that man's head into a fender? Why did I have to do all the things in Quentin that I needed to so I could survive my time? Why—

Wait.

That was it.

Harding was giving me permission to chisel into my humungous confusion: my eye. What I did to my eye was the thing I couldn't understand the most in this litany of un-understandable enterprises. I needed to write toward the unanswerable: How could I do that to myself?

It was time for the graduating man, Elio, to read his piece to the group. He'd gotten sent up for stealing a motorcycle to use as getaway wheels for a bank robbery. He scoped out a branch that was near some windy back roads and knew a cop car didn't stand a chance chasing him through the curves at top speed. Problem was a couple was out walking on that quiet lane, and Elio clipped the man, injuring him only slightly, while Elio and the bike slid on the asphalt for fifty feet, before being launched into a ravine. Now he walked with a cane and had scars on the right side of his body from the ankle to his shoulder, where the road bit off his skin.

Now it was obvious Elio didn't want to read the story, but it was also obvious that Harding usually got his way.

"Just fucking read," said Harding.

"I don't think I can," Elio said.

"Why not?"

"Because I don't want all you to know so much about me."

"It's a great story." Then Harding spoke to us: "It has magic in it, and Elio is worried that you guys might—"

"Call me a huge pussy," said Elio.

"I dig stories about magic," I said to him. "So if you're a huge pussy, so am I."

A few other halfway heads mustered grunts of corroboration—yup, they were also huge pussies—and so Elio did the thing that scared the shit out of him: He showed us his heart.

He stood in front of us, leaning on his cane, the pages in his other hand wobbling with nerves. "I got busted when your mom was pregnant," he read to us, "but she didn't know that yet. Only a month along or so. If she don't know, I don't know. So I get sent up for five years, and I get this letter from her saying that she won't visit. Not with you growing inside her body. And she won't budge on it. She said she won't come because the baby would remember meeting me in prison, and it would poison her. Kids shouldn't be on the inside of these institutions, she told me. So I was going to be locked up the whole pregnancy and the first years of her life, and they weren't going to visit me. I couldn't visit them. So I needed to come up with a different way to see them. Okay, I started folding these little dolls out of pages I ripped from books. I made hundreds of them. It started that I was going to make one and mail it to my kid, but they didn't look good at first. So I kept folding them up, kept making them. I didn't know what my old lady was having, boy or girl, so I made two colors of dolls, pink and blue. For the pink, I used ketchup and my spit to dilute it down, and the blue was just pen, but I also cut it with spit to lighten it. I know these days people get pissed about boy shit versus girl shit, but fuck it, I'll give them options so if the boy wants the pink one and the girl, the blue, so be it. Who gives a shit? I just want them to be played with. I just want to know that this doll that I made in the joint found its way into her little hand and it made her happy. And then one night I was up late on my bunk folding a batch of new dolls, and I got a paper cut, a deep one, and I bled from the tip of my index finger and a drop landed splat, right on the pink doll, right on the doll's chest. In fact, the drop of blood looked like a heart. At first, I was pissed. I'd ruined the doll—and right as I was about to crumple the bloody thing, the paper heart started beating. I'm serious. Then the doll sat up and introduced itself as Haley. *I can go meet your baby for you and tell you what I learn,* she offered. I agreed and watched the doll run from the cell, and it took three days for Haley to come back. A three-day root canal. The doll told me that my baby was a girl. That you should be born next month. The doll said that your mom was thinking about naming you Ava. It fucking burns not being involved, not being asked what names I like. Not many letters, and the ones that come are filled with small talk. It is so fucking lonely to make small talk with someone who you still love, but now you're wondering if they might not love you back. Haley said she could go ask your mom. If I really wanted to know the truth. Of course I wanted the truth. Who wouldn't want the truth about their own family? And so the doll left again, and it took her even longer to return this time, a few months, and the span of time was one long colonoscopy, hold the opiates. I couldn't sleep. I couldn't remember shit. I was talking to myself more. I was incensed when the doll finally returned, demanded to know what took her so long. I told Haley how much anguish had sloshed around my cell these last months, and the doll started crying. *What? What's wrong?* The doll didn't want to tell me. But I insisted. I had to hear. It would've been faster if she'd just hit me with a bat. My girlfriend wasn't my girlfriend anymore. There was a new man. And Ava came out eight pounds two ounces, and these two girls who were not mine, and this man who now had a family with them, they ate pancakes for breakfast, went on vacations to the Grand Canyon, wore matching fucking jerseys during the Super Bowl. And Haley offered to keep helping me, offered to keep tabs on Ava, to learn more about her and report back intimate details. Her personality, her hobbies. And the doll was only trying to be supportive, but if you were made of paper and there was only one drop of blood in your heart, you didn't get it. You didn't understand that these next broadcasts would destroy me. That doll couldn't comprehend how hearing these things was building a prison in a prison. And I could only be locked inside of so many walls before I went mad. So please understand, Ava, that I did want to know you. I did want to be your dad. That was why I made the dolls. Did you ever get them? Did you ever play with them? I'm sorry if the pink ones smell like ketchup. I'm sorry

I went to prison. The doll wanted to set off back to you to begin these reports, but I wouldn't let her go. I grabbed the doll. I held Haley in my palm like a baby bird. The doll looked at me. I apologized to her. For the first time, she was scared—and that was fair, because I was terrified of her, of how Haley could hammer me on to a cross, how every new report would drive the spikes deeper into my hands and feet. And then for some reason my hand starts folding in on Haley as she sits in my palm, and she tells me that I'm hurting her, that I'm crushing her. The doll wants to know why I'd kill something I made from scratch, but it's either her or me. We can't both be here. The doll screams, the paper doll dying in my hand, a heap of warped limbs, a final crumple, and the doll is dead. I hope you have a good life, Ava. I hope you get to be one of the few people who are actually happy here."

M

The next morning, Cassidy sped the 'Vette east toward the Merry Days development where Jacques claimed Mom Jon lived. The temperature was already in the triple digits as we slid deeper into this scorched country of fast-food mirages and gas stations every twenty miles.

"Captain Romance," she said, "taking me to kidnap an old lady."

"We're not kidnapping her."

"Uh-huh."

"We're rescuing her."

"If you say so."

I hadn't gotten a wink of sleep, and I was already in a battle trance. Couldn't sleep 'cause I couldn't trust Jacques, and since Val at Slide City told me he pushed pills, I didn't know who else he worked with or for, or who watched his six. There was no way to predict the push-back I might get grabbing Mom Jon, so I was going to storm this village with all my berserker charm.

We were in Burned Dirt, California, no life in any direction you looked, except the highway swarm of people trying to speed through the desolation at all costs. Toxic, Martian, flat. You broke down out here, in this heat, you might burst into flames before the tow truck showed up to scoop your bones. With nothing but dirt, the world felt like a dream about boredom.

By the time we arrived it was 107 degrees. The Merry Days was a petri dish of new life plopped in the middle of a septic planet. A fetus in a barren womb.

"Do you feel that charge in the air?" I asked Cassidy.

"It feels like it did back in the tube slide with the ghosts," she said. "It feels like we're surrounded by them."

I couldn't get a clear line of sight on the houses in the Merry Days yet because the entire subdivision had a grove of wind turbines running around it, a huge rectangle of them as a perimeter. Almost like castle walls. The propellers weren't turning on the turbines, though they weren't totally still, either, shuddering in the breeze like broken metronomes, eking out desperate, impossible rhythms. They made dry honking noises like swans dying of thirst.

The windows in the Corvette were rolled down, and as we neared the gates to the Merry Days, these turbines serenaded us, like Geiger counters, farts of noise to signal nuclear radiation. So we found the entrance and drove the Corvette into Chernobyl West.

There was no one outside any of these new houses. There were no cars parked in driveways. No sign of residents: no flags out front, no delivery boxes, no toys in front yards, no bikes, no gardens, no pets. Slowly, we cruised down the middle of the desolation.

"Where is everyone?" I asked Cassidy.

"Maybe we can't see them," she said. "If they're ghosts, I mean."

"That's a really scary thing to say," I said. "It would make a good movie."

"Cheap to make, if your actors are ghosts."

"That's the place," and I pointed to a two-story house coming up on the left. Yet another spot with no sign of life out front. And I couldn't see in the windows. They were all blacked out. Entirely. But that address matched what Jacques had said.

"Don't pull into the driveway," I said to her. "Park at the curb."

The breeze picked up some, and the wind turbines honked louder. Were they warning me? Or were they the witches who watched over the Merry Days? Or maybe Cassidy was right, and we were surrounded by ghosts, and they were having invisible barbecues and washing their ghost-mobiles, and their kids dove into swimming pools filled with melted ice cream, and we simply couldn't see their joys.

But none of that mattered. I was on a mission for Mom Jon.

I had a foot of pipe and a ten-inch knife.

The heart in my chest was huge.

For a minute, I remembered that everyone had a soul, and we were all scared.

Then that minute ended, and it was time to go in. A Viking would never say something as greeting card as "better safe than sorry," but we operated under a similar rule: Have weapons. Be ready.

Cassidy parked the 'Vette, and we got out. I walked to the trunk, and Cassidy's face startled. "Oh. I totally forgot he was back there," she said.

"I did, too, for a good stretch of the drive."

"He's probably super hot," she said.

We popped it open to see Jacques staring back at us with wide eyes and rhubarb-red cheeks, gleaming with ruddy conviction. Our silhouettes, from his perspective, must've looked like giant monsters.

"I am a changed man!" he said to us, as though he'd been expecting us to pop the trunk right that very second, this preordained reveal for his declaration. "I am a changed man who is seeing the world for the first time!"

"Heatstroke," Cassidy said to me, "or did he find God?"

"What's the difference?" I asked.

"It is much easier to cure heatstroke," she said.

"I'm letting all the venom of this world go," he said to us. "I'm free from all the poison. I'm running on clean energy. How about you?"

"Unfortunately, that sounds a lot like religion," Cassidy said to me.

I said to him, "Get your wits, or I'll hit you in the face."

He wiped the enlightened lather from his brain and face. "Oh. Right. You. I'm listening to whatever you say," he said.

"That's good thinking," I said.

"When I first woke up," he said, "I didn't know this was a trunk."

"Where did you think you were?"

"A lot of places."

"Like?"

"I thought maybe I'd shrunk down, and this was a dollhouse. But I could always hear my father's voice, for some reason. He wanted me to clean out the closet."

"How long until you put it together that you were in a trunk?"

He lowered his head in shame. "I didn't. Not until you threw it open."

"You were reborn in the trunk of a Corvette?" Cassidy laughed. "That's the white-trashiest book of the Bible I've ever fucking heard. The Book of Jacques."

"I feel silly now," he said.

"Game face," I said to Jacques. "I need to know what I'm walking into."

"You're walking into the cleanest house that's ever existed," he said.

"What does that mean?"

"It's all she does," he said. "She never finishes cleaning because she never remembers starting."

"And you just let her clean up all the time?"

"It makes her happy," he said. "Go see for yourself."

I was having trouble getting my legs to work. "It's possible she won't know me," I said to him.

"Or she might think you're somebody else."

"She does that with you?"

"It's a big problem."

"I'll tell you what your problems are," I said, "once I talk to Mom Jon."

"Don't let her make you coffee. Her coffee is terrible."

"Any weapons in there?"

"There's a gun under the kitchen sink. One in the sock drawer."

"A dog?"

"No dog. Will you relax? You're going to walk in the door and find her dusting a shelf or something. She'll be listening to Joni Mitchell. And whether you want to believe it or not, she'll have a smile on her face."

I looked at the house again. "And why can't I see in the windows?"

"It's just how they're tinted from the outside. It's nothing. You'll see. Go knock and she'll let you in."

"And nobody else is in there," I said. "Say it one more time, and I'll choke you to death if you lie."

"She is alone. I promise," said Jacques, the man I couldn't trust.

"I'm going to shut you in the trunk again," I said.

Cassidy climbed back in the Corvette to stand guard, and right as I went to slam the trunk, Jacques said eagerly, "I can't wait to find out what I see in here this time!"

ᛗ

I had a foot of pipe in my left hand.

I had a ten-inch knife in my right.

I walked slowly up toward the house with its blackened windows, feeling my ancestors. They were ready to light up the world with fire, and the closer I got, it was obvious that it wasn't tinting. No. It was pure black. The windows had been painted over.

I shot around and looked back at the Corvette, and Cassidy said, "What?" and I said, "Your gun. Get it out. Keep it on your lap."

"What is it?" she said.

"It's fucking wrong," I said.

I walked slowly up the path. I stood at the front door, knocked with the butt of the knife. Hid the weapons behind my back. Smiled pleasantly in case an eye perused me through the peephole.

And that was what happened. "Who is it?" Mom Jon said through the door.

Finally, her voice! There was no way I'd mistake that. Not a chance. It was her. She was in there.

The quivering propellers of the wind turbines sounded like cellos begging for mercy.

"Mom Jon?" I said. "It's me. It's James."

"Who?"

"James. Rebecca's nephew. We used to live together in the Lower Haight."

"Are you here to help with the light bulbs? I've been waiting for three days for the light bulb people."

She might not remember me by name, but I had to know what she would see if she opened the door, if I wasn't a small man through a peephole, if we stood face-to-face. So I said, "I'm sorry for the wait, ma'am. We've been slammed. It's a busy time in the light bulb business."

She opened the door. There wasn't a light on inside. I couldn't see anything back behind her. All I could see was her huge body in dirty underwear and an open bathrobe, and for some reason, she wore a ski jacket over the robe. She had the look of somebody who'd put their brain in the basket of a hot-air balloon and watched it float off.

And just because she didn't show up for me in Quentin, that didn't mean I couldn't rise to the occasion, didn't mean that I couldn't be better to her than she was to me. I needed to do the thing she couldn't: follow a loved one into the darkness.

"Are you okay?" I said to her.

"Light bulbs," said Mom Jon, "they got us by the balls, right?"

"Who's got us by the balls?" I asked.

"The light bulb–industrial complex," she said. "I know they butter your bread, but come on, even you must see what they're up to."

"I've got one good eye," I said.

"This is a world without light bulbs, so you're seeing better than most."

"Is something wrong with your power?" I said. "I can check it for you."

"Electricity's fine. It's just these light bulbs. They won't stay lit. But don't worry. There is hope in the kitchen. Would you like to see our hope?"

There was a switch on the wall, and I reached in and flipped it up, but the room remained pitch. The house's AC, however, was clearly functioning, and I felt its cool breeze on my face.

"Come on, I'll take you to ground zero," she said, and retreated into the dark house. In a matter of seconds, I couldn't see her.

"Wait," I said, remaining at the door, "is anybody here with you?"

"Who?"

"Is anyone else here?"

"Who's here?" she said.

I groaned. "You really don't recognize me?" I called after her.

She didn't answer.

"Mom Jon! Are you alone?"

"I don't know you," the voice came back from the black. And there was nothing for a few seconds. Then, from somewhere in that deep space: "Let me show you the hope!"

Then all the wind turbines began to spin at once, the propellers yawning, squawking, speed building, and the ambient moan of the blades jostling. Soon, the sky sounded like it was running through a distortion pedal. I pulled the knife out from behind my back and stepped inside the dark house.

I couldn't see anything the farther in I went. It was darker than the tube slide. Darker than Jacques's trunk. I used my phone's flashlight, walked slowly, careful not to stumble into a trap. The walls were papered with missing children posters running from floor to ceiling.

There was a unicycle and bicycle parked in the living room, their frames catching the flashlight spookily. Right past them, a motorcycle.

What wheeled contraption would come next? Another motorcycle, this one without wheels or a gas tank. I turned a corner and, way off down a long hall, saw light. The kitchen.

Mom Jon had the refrigerator door propped open.

"Planned obsolescence!" she said. "Everything they sell us is wired to fry. It's broken before we ring the register. They don't want us seeing nothing, these light bulb fucks."

Mom Jon's massive body was plopped on the floor in front of the open fridge. She was using the light in there to read a paperback, which explained the jacket she wore.

"See," she said to me, as I inched closer to her, "the refrigerator people don't play by the rules. They care."

"Are you hungry, Mom Jon?" I asked, putting my knife away. "When was the last time you ate?"

"Fridge people are in the business of feeding people, so they have heart. That's why light bulbs in refrigerators last longer than the ones in the rest of the house. The people in charge of the rest of the rooms are all monsters. But there is hope here in the fridge."

"What about some water?" I said to her. "Are you thirsty?"

"So do you think you'll be able to help me with the rest of the light bulbs, young man? We need to be able to see better," she said to me. "We need to know where to go."

"Okay. You stay here," I said, "and I'll look around and see what I can do."

"Why do you have that big knife?" she asked.

"Protection. I'm worried about you, and I want to keep you safe."

"I'm safe. Cold, is all. I'm cold on account of sitting in front of this fridge."

"I'll see about fixing the lights."

"Hey, you're nice, you know that? You're real nice." She tugged me on the arm, then pointed toward the ceiling, toward the house's second story. Then she whispered, "Not nice."

"Who's up there?"

She pointed to the ceiling again. "That demon slaps me."

NOT NICE.

Now these were new circumstances.

I was ready to overreact.

In moments like this, I always found it handy to go berserker, to not just put yourself in harm's way but ingest it, become it, feel the harm's way swim in your blood. Tattoo it on your forehead. My head was harm's halfway house.

I needed to go see about a not-nice demon. I hopped on the motorcycle in the hall, turned the key, kicked it in the ribs to fill it with rage, and I rode this horse and squealed it up the stairs. At the top, a man appeared in a doorway at the other end of a narrow hall, a man who I assumed was this demon who slapped her, a man who kept her in the dark, naked, crazed, a man who was now frozen in the doorway, who didn't know how much worse it was about to get for him, and right then, I let go of the motorcycle, and I rolled off the back of the bike and watched it soar down the hall and crash into the man, leveling him before he could get out of the way, the bike smashing past him and into the back wall of the far bedroom, the man screaming as loud as the downed bike.

I sped into the room, too, killed the still-running engine, fell on top of the man, my knee in his stomach, my knife at his throat. "Talk," I said.

"Where's my brother?" he said, giving me the side-eye.

"Is anyone else in the house?"

"Is he dead?"

I knocked Side-Eye on the forehead with the butt of the knife.

"No one's here!" he said.

"Jacques is your brother?"

"Yeah."

"He's fine. Outside."

"Oh fuck, my leg!"

I wouldn't dare describe to you the meat scene of his butchered leg. Whatever you were imagining, it was worse.

"There will be a lot of physical therapy," I said.

"I keep waiting for it to stop hurting so much," he said through a series of short gasps.

"Your pill connection will come in handy." I bumped Side-Eye on the forehead again with the butt of the knife. "Whom do you work for?"

He was happy to talk due to the shock, which was like sodium pentothal; he couldn't answer my questions fast enough, catching up like old pals. Side-Eye was the younger of the two brothers. (Dimmer, though he didn't say that. That was me interjecting.) The brothers had a deal with a pill mill, using their skydiving school for deliveries and as a cover story.

"That's it, man," he said. "We fly product for them."

"Flew."

"What?"

"You are no longer the owner of a functioning plane."

"What happened to it?"

"It burned," I said.

"How?"

"Me."

"You?"

"Yeah, I burned it."

He screamed even louder now, like the news hurt worse than the broken leg. "If that's true, our partners are going to kill us." He was staring around me at the carnage that was his leg. "They'll kill us . . . like, for real."

He arched his back trying to buck me off, and he immediately yelled with anguish and fell back, supine, dejected. It wasn't resignation because I was sitting on him. I could tell that right away. It was resignation as he anticipated the wrath of his partners.

"Now tell me what's going on with Mom Jon," I said to him, and adjusted the knife at his throat.

Maybe you didn't know what it was like to hold a knife to a man's neck.

Maybe you didn't know what it was like to hold a knife to a man's neck who hurt someone you loved.

Here was the story Side-Eye told: The brothers had just bought this whole subdivision with their pill money. They had ambitions to use the vacants as labs to make their own drugs someday but were still saving up seed money. It was becoming a theme: more mismanagement of perfectly good real estate! Some of what Jacques had said was confirmed by his brother: He and Mom Jon fought hard and lived hard. The brothers had been living off the grid at Slide City, as cheap as possible, saving to buy the subdivision. They'd been moving product successfully, and they holed up here last month. Things were right on schedule.

But there was another schedule, too. Another clock. One that Side-Eye didn't know about at first. See, over the last eight months, Jacques did the one thing that could jeopardize this probable future of theirs. He started gobbling pills. And these pills were fun at first, and Jacques had these fun times right in front of Mom Jon, who thought, *Hey, I also enjoy fun times*, and so she began gobbling pills. These fun times came with fine print, too tiny for dilated pupils, and so they didn't understand that soon, the fun times would both dull and grow more urgent simultaneously. That you would want to chase the high of those first fun times with fanatical terror and devotion. Because what if you never found them again? What if you never knew that kind of pleasure? Could you survive such a crushing fate? And the more you looked, the hazier it all got, and you couldn't remember if it was day or night, and your emotions were liquidated for pennies on the dollar, and the only person who sent you a birthday card was an old and greedy dentist. The pills, for some reason, worked different on Mom Jon. They tangled her memories into a nest of old guitar cables. According to Side-Eye, she had conversations with people in 1979 and 1985 and 1998. At the same time. She joked with an invisible friend that she was a quantum ninja. Side-Eye heard her say to a confidant that she once bounced Einstein on her knee and called him a good boy with potential. She couldn't stop talking out loud to this hysterical ensemble. This was what led to so many fights in the house. All these conversations she'd have with invisible friends. All these screaming matches across space-time. She was living in a different world from the brothers', but they were all under one roof. She was a satellite picking up too many signals, and she couldn't stop talking out loud and it drove the brothers nuts. Jacques stuffed more pills in his ears to get away from her racket, so Side-Eye had to solve the problem. He noticed that she was quieter at night, and when he asked her about it, she said, "The dark makes them sleepy, so it's peaceful in the dark." So he hit the fuse box eight days ago. Killed the power. Saved the AC. She'd been in a blackout ever since. The fridge they ran on a generator, so the food didn't spoil.

"Are you keeping Mom Jon here against her will?" I said to Side-Eye.

Even though I was mounted on top of him with a knife to his throat, he looked at me like I was an idiot. "Did you hear what I just told you?" he asked. "She was making me crazy. I hoped she'd leave today and yesterday and the one before that. Here against her will? I'd drive her to the bus station myself, right now, buy her a ticket to anywhere."

"What about your brother? He sounds like the kind of man who says he loves you while drugging your drink."

"What they have only makes sense to them," said Side-Eye. "I know he's a piece of shit for scrapping with her. I know I am, too."

"I will give you your brother back," I said, "and I'm taking Mom Jon."

"Our plane is really gone?" he asked.

"Yes."

"And you're taking her for real?"

"Yeah."

"And my leg is pretty bad?"

"Uh-huh."

"And they're gonna kill us?"

"Well, you seem to think so," I said, "and since I don't know them, I'm just telling you what you told me."

"This is a terrible day," he said.

"Leave town. Now."

"I can't walk."

"I can," I said, and got off him, stood up straight. I tucked the knife in the back of my jeans. "I can walk right out and leave you to it."

"Leave me to what?"

"Wait for your business associates."

"Hey!" he said. "Don't leave me up here!" but I shut the door to his room, leaving him with the wrecked bike and busted leg.

He yelled at me as I walked to the stairs, down them, back into the kitchen to grab Mom Jon. She was still reading her paperback by the light of the fridge, sitting there in her jacket, her open robe. "Who are you?" she asked.

I was so close to her. We were so close. We could have hugged, could've kissed on the cheek. We could've danced or sang. There were so many things we could do if only she knew who I was.

I had to keep trying.

She was still in there.

I'd keep trying because I wasn't in a cage.

I'd keep trying because she had looked after me.

We still knew each other; somehow, I was sure of that.

Right?

And could you understand how her amnesia made me as lost as my happy monster? Mom Jon was the only family I had left, and she didn't remember me. And maybe it was her brain dying or maybe it was the drugs, but I was going to find out for sure. Then, as her wits came back online, we'd know the truth. But that was for tomorrow, and the next day, and the next. Now, all I knew was this: We were two humans standing in the light of the fridge.

So I tried again: "Do you remember your old poetry readings? Do you remember the dirt stage?" I searched her face for any recognition, but she was somewhere else. The pills made her a ghost to herself. Or I hoped it was only the pills. "You made this stage where people went to be themselves, Mom Jon. You freed a lot of people. I watched it. I've missed you. I wished you visited me more."

She didn't say anything at first. Finally, after about five seconds of staring, she said, "A dirt stage? That sounds nice."

M

I was excited to get to the trunk, wanted to hear where Jacques had gone this time. Had he changed again? Did he fly off on quests that only he could see? I couldn't wait to vault into his mythic adventures, and so I popped the trunk with the enthusiasm of a boy tearing open a gift.

But he was dead.

That wasn't good.

His eyes were shut. He was super flushed, the color of brick.

"This isn't good," I said to Cassidy, who still sat behind the Corvette's wheel.

She stuck her head out the window. "What?"

"It seems," I said, "that Jacques has died."

She got out and joined me by the back, and we stared down at the body in the trunk. Then she spoke with the neutral tone of somebody disassociating: "Huh. I guess we did that."

"Really, it's the sun's fault," I said.

"The State of California might disagree," Cassidy said. "This fucking world. If there isn't a Tony shaving your eyebrows, there's a dead Jacques in your trunk."

"Don't worry. We can carry him inside, set the place on fire," I said, which I tried to bring into the conversation as a helpful suggestion. Cassidy's gaze, however, implied a more negative interpretation of my contribution.

"It concerns me how quickly that dawned on you," she said.

"He's dead, Cassidy."

"I'm not saying it's a bad idea," she said. "It came fast, that's all."

Then the corpse of Jacques sat up, bending stiff at the waste, like a car trunk Frankenstein's monster. Gasping for air, he reached out toward us.

"And that's why you don't light someone on fire," Cassidy said to me.

"I know what happens when we die!" he announced.

"What?" asked Cassidy.

"I don't want to know," I said.

"We go somewhere warm."

"You mean like hell?" Cassidy asked.

He collapsed in the trunk again, out cold. We carried Jacques inside, and he woke as we dumped him on the couch. He immediately stripped down to his undies and got in the fetal position, started talking again: "After you die, it feels like sunbathing. Still and relaxed."

"So more like heaven?" Cassidy said to him.

"Just, like, *warm*," he said. "So you can dance all night."

"You're talking about a trunk," I said.

"But just because the weather's pretty," he said, "that doesn't mean there isn't a devil. It's been my experience that devils live everywhere."

"The fluffy horseshit he talks," Cassidy said to me, "makes it impossible to tell the difference between heaven and hell."

Jacques tucked his head down into his fetal shell and said, "I hear the devil right now." Then he started mumbling fast, sprawling paragraphs of gibberish for just him and the devil, his unreleased album, his banned book, his stolen jewel, his robbed grave, his masterpiece lost at sea, the last print of a classic film charred in a warehouse fire.

"Who's down there?" Side-Eye called from upstairs. "Help! I need help!"

Jacques didn't hear him, but we did. We heard Side-Eye, and we didn't care. To me, he was just another CO abusing an inmate, and he could yell all day and night, and I'd never help him for how he treated Mom Jon. That was how we left the brothers, on different stories in a house in the Merry Days tract, waiting for their pill partners to come for blood.

Or maybe these shady brothers would cockroach their way out of danger. Maybe they'd go on to fly their drugs across the sky. Or maybe this was the day that turned them around. They went cold turkey, kicked this life, turned into someone else. You never knew. That was their saga to write, not mine.

As for us, we got back in the Corvette and left the Merry Days behind.

TAKING MOM JON HOME wasn't as simple as depositing her in Unit 12, kicking the invaders out, claiming our land back. First order of business was her brain, her health. We needed to know who she was without skag. And *we* didn't mean Cassidy and me. *We* meant the white coats. Neither Cassidy nor I would be confused with a neurologist, and that was who Mom Jon needed.

If we dropped her at an ER, they'd help her kick in a more controlled way than I could. It was still going to be a crash landing and those never felt good, but maybe the doctors and nurses knew how to ease the agonies. Hopefully, they'd be empathic and patient and full of grace, with an innate sense that someone wonderful was stuck under Mom Jon's drugs, but my gut told me those who worked in emergency didn't care about addicts. Maybe they did at one time, earlier in their careers, but since then, they'd seen so many junkies beg them for help, only to be back there a few weeks later begging for the same help, returning yet again, never getting straight, never taking any accountability, and after that happened enough times, these doctors and nurses grew to resent or even hate junkies for wasting their time—*Why should their self-destruction be our everlasting problem?*—and so they were stingy with these resources, hydration, numbing agents, precisely because they wanted you to feel it, wanted withdrawal to hurt, and maybe, if they really let you live in that inferno for a few days, maybe, just maybe, you finally tried not to come back.

Still, I had no other choice. I couldn't take care of her and spend every night away sleeping at the halfway house. I needed to convince myself they'd show her mercy. That was how she could get help, and I could live with myself.

I started that process by driving from the Merry Days to a drugstore, where I bought Comet, fancy lotions, shampoo, and conditioner. Cassidy helped me pick out some makeup. I also got a sundress and some flip-flops, which, as you knew from Python Wally, was not my favorite fashion choice. But I wanted her to be comfortable.

We went from the drugstore to a motel, where I dug a sponge into the tub, scrubbing it to a gleam, good as new, showroom ready. I drew a hot bath and dumped bubbles into it. I helped Mom Jon strip, and I held her hand as she got into the bath. She laid back gingerly and then submerged herself entirely beneath the hot water. For several beats she remained under the surface, before finally coming back up to breathe.

Sitting on the closed toilet in the small motel bathroom, I rubbed shampoo into her scalp, and she rinsed. I rubbed the conditioner in, and she rinsed. I was taking care of her, and I was happy. She was getting clean, and she looked happy, too.

"Where are we?" she said.

"We are getting you ready to go."

"Where am I going?"

"Somebody wants to help you."

"I can tell you who doesn't want to help us," she said. "Trees."

"Trees?"

"Trees fucking hate us," she said, "and they'll turn on us the first chance they get."

I opened a new brush from its packaging. "Do you mind if I run this brush through your hair?"

"That sounds nice," she said. "Wait. What were we just talking about? Something about nature?"

I combed through the ends of her hair slowly. This would be the only easy part. The rest was unkempt, knotting. "You were talking about how trees hate us."

Her eyes grew wide: "We treat the Garden of Eden like a rest stop bathroom, so fuck us. We deserve what we're gonna get."

I grabbed her hair with some slack, so I wouldn't hurt her scalp. Squirting in more conditioner, I tried to ease through the knots, the tangles, the thorns.

"Am I hurting you?" I asked her.

"I'm a tough old broad," she said.

"Let me know if it hurts."

"You're nice."

One of the snarls gave, and the brush went through smoothly. "You were one of the people who taught me to be nice," I said to her. "You did that for me, and I'll never forget it."

"So that's where we are," she said.

"Where are we?"

"You pulled me into your dream."

"How do you know this is a dream?" I asked.

"Because your skin's purple, and I can see your heart glowing through it."

And I thought, *Now that's how you give a compliment.*

Also I thought, *Mom Jon, it's my pleasure to bring you back to life.*

"I'm going to start brushing again," I said, grabbing her hair gently, going to work on another clump, and this time, the brush hacked through the hair more easily. "I want to take you home," I said, "but first, we need to make sure you're healthy."

"Every animal is as healthy as they need to be," she said, "and then we die. We think we're more important because we run the zoos. But until they give giraffes routine breast exams, medicine's just hubris."

"Not everything needs to kill us," I said.

"Sure, it does."

"No."

"I like it," she said, "you brushing my hair."

"Do you remember me?"

"Yeah," she said, "you're with the light bulb people."

"From before that."

"Before the light bulb, there was only darkness."

"We used to love each other," I said. "Maybe we still do."

"Dreaming boy," she said to me.

Her hair was brushed straight, gray strands stuck to her freckled back, a faded tattoo of what was once Earth on her shoulder blade, but thanks to the minefields of time, it looked like a milky eye, an entire world where no one could see. She'd been looking away from me while I worked on her hair, and now, she turned and stared, studying me like I was the clouds, like she was looking for order in the froth.

"I know you can't answer this question," I said, "but I need to ask it anyway: Do you know where my guitar is?"

"Have you asked an iPhone?" she said. "They're filled with online scams and porn, but maybe they can help you."

"Let's dry you off." And I helped her out of the tub, patted her body, her hair, her tattooed and trashed Earth. She changed into the sundress, slid into the flip-flops, and sat on the motel bed while Cassidy did her makeup.

"In this dream, we must be traveling to a very important world for you to go to all this trouble," she said.

"You are going to a world that can see inside you. They can take pictures of you. Make sure you're okay."

"Aren't you coming?"

"You won't be alone there," I said. "I'll visit you. Every day."

Then she rocketed up to standing: "I need to pee," and I backed out of the bathroom, and she slammed the door.

"I'll do for you what you couldn't do for me," I whispered to the shut door, knowing she couldn't hear me.

ᛗ

We pulled up to the ER about three in the afternoon. Cassidy hit the brakes. Mom Jon was on my lap in the 'Vette's passenger seat.

"Park around the corner," I said to Cassidy. "I'll be there in a few minutes."

I opened the passenger door, and Mom Jon climbed out into a sunny afternoon. I was right behind her and told her to sit next to a hedge by the ashtrays. "Who is it?" she said of the hedge.

"Ask it," I said.

"I try not to talk to trees I don't know."

"That's a hedge."

"What is this place?" Mom Jon said.

"It's how we see inside you," I said.

"I was talking to the hedge," she said to me. Then her face turned serious, speaking to the hedge directly: "Oh. It's over, huh?"

All three of us—me, Mom Jon, the hedge—were silent.

Then I said, "What's over?"

"Your dream," said Mom Jon. "It's ending."

"Stay here," I said. "I'll be right back," and I went inside and spoke to a security guard. "There is a woman out front," I told him. "She isn't making sense."

"You know her?"

"No," I said, "but something's not right with her. She is talking to a hedge."

"Super," said Security, fifty pounds too light to be working the job. "I'll send somebody out to deal with it."

"Her."

"What?"

"Deal with her," I said, "not it."

"I meant the hedge situation, not the person."

"I'm not trying to crawl up your ass."

"Yeah, you did. We're always on the verge of turning on each other," he said. "That's the world."

He sighed, looked toward the exit, and radioed it in. We exited together through the automatic doors, and I pointed at Mom Jon. He nodded and walked closer, and soon a couple more security guards and nurses were outside, too.

"Excuse me, ma'am?" I heard him say, and they wrestled her into the wheelchair.

"Where are you taking me?" she asked, and she fought them. She screamed at them. And then she did the worst thing: She looked over at me, wanting help, wanting the one thing I couldn't do. She didn't understand that we needed them. They were the only way to know the truth. And yet the idea that I was the one locking her up made me want to drive the Corvette into a wall at a hundred miles an hour, and as my skull exploded, my last thought would be: *This is exactly what you deserve for abandoning your people.*

I'm sorry, Mom Jon, but I couldn't see another way to help except leaving you.

Was that why you never visited me in Quentin? Did you need to leave me to help me?

I hoped to have the opportunity to ask her in the future.

And perhaps, because her memories were all stepped-on grenades, she wouldn't even remember what was going on as they dragged her into emergency. But I'd remember. I'd always hear her screaming as they led her away, while I stood there like a coward.

Whatever else happened as they rolled her through the doors into the hospital, the rest of this wasn't for me. This part had too many teeth. I had to get out of there, or I wouldn't go through with it. She needed help and I was leaving her, and I was doing the right thing, and I was doing the right thing, and I was doing the right thing, and I was doing the right thing.

I got back to the 'Vette in twenty seconds, that last look in her eyes, that confusion, chasing after me, a suicide bomb of guilt.

"Is she okay?" Cassidy asked.

"Will you break my nose?"

"What?"

"Will you please punch me in the face?"

Most people, on reflex, would say no.

They'd say, *Of course not.*

Or: *Why the fuck do you want me to do that?*

Or: *I can't hurt you like that.*

But Cassidy wasn't most people, and I knew she'd understand that I wasn't asking her to hurt me; I was asking if she'd give me CPR, give me stitches, a stent, a tracheotomy, a kidney, a hand, a heart, a lifeline, a rescue, a panic room, a palace. I was only asking her if she could hit my face and shake my brain and quiet the beehive of leaving Mom Jon. Yes, Cassidy would hit me in the nose. I knew she'd do that, and even if her punch didn't break it, the violence would achieve the desired effect, making a fizz in my head, a carbonation behind the eyes, so I could feel buzzy, amnesiac, perfect.

Instead, however, Cassidy said, "No, I won't hit you in the face."

That was disappointing to hear.

"Come on, why not?" I asked.

"Because I won't."

"Why not?"

"Because that's not what you need."

"What do I need?"

"I'm about to show you," she said.

"THE SHOW STARTS SOON," CASSIDY SAID.

We'd parked the 'Vette right outside the business's storefront. We were back in the city, in the Castro, and the exterior of the building was covered in a mural of vines and gourds, greens and oranges bragging vibrant colors. It made it seem like there was life teeming, but the building also had bars on its windows.

"What is this place?" I asked.

"An after-school program that my friend runs. It's for elementary-age kids with Down syndrome."

Right then, a woman came out front carrying two big garbage bags, and a man followed behind hauling a ladder. The man arranged the ladder, and then the woman climbed it, holding those big black plastic bags. About halfway up, she heaved them on the roof, then she finished her climb.

"So what's in the bags?" I asked.

"You don't need to be punched," said Cassidy, "you need to watch this."

Cassidy and I sat in the 'Vette. Our parking meter was broken, which meant it was free, or put another way, meant to be. And sitting in this moment with Cassidy, something appeared to me.

"I wrote something for you," I said.

"When?"

"Right now."

"You wrote it down where?"

"In my head."

"You wrote it down in your head?"

"And now I want to tell it you."

"I mean, technically," she said, "all talking is really just telling somebody something you wrote in your head."

"This is different. I wrote you a letter."

"A head letter."

"It starts," I said, "like this: Dear Cassidy."

"Old-school."

"Dear Cassidy," I said, "I'm contacting you today in regard to your suggestion of Being Careful . . ."

Right then, the front door blew open from the after-school program, and about ten kids ran out, smiling and looking up to the sky, excited. Another woman trailed the children, saw Cassie sitting in the car, smiled, waved. Everyone gazed up to the roof, and right then, the lady on the roof reached into one of the garbage bags and threw a burst of flower petals into the air, a swarm of them, fat and clumsy, sashaying in the San Francisco gray.

"That woman up there," Cassidy said, "is a florist, and she does this with the kids a couple times a week. Collecting all the petals from her shop, making these snowstorms for them to play in. I come watch as often as I can. I don't really know why. I just know that I always leave in a better mood. You could use a cheer-up."

The florist rained down handfuls of petals, and the kids danced.

"This is what you wanted to show me?" I asked.

"This beats a punch in the face any day, right?"

The florist then turned the first bag over and shook it out, creating a flurry.

"Keep going," Cassidy said. "Tell me the whole head letter."

"Right. Back to business. The next part goes like this: First off, I am absolutely interested in entering a phase of my life that would champion a more measured approach, and I'm hoping that, quite soon, I'll be able to abide by that."

The kids reached for the falling flower petals. I could hear them laugh. A girl was singing, "*It's raining, it's pouring,*" and one kid hopped on another for a piggyback ride. They joyfully braved these elements, these storms from a garden. The florist was really going now, both her fists throwing rapid-fire flowers.

"I don't know a lot about business, Cassidy," I said, "but I've heard that sometimes it takes a certain window of time while contracts are finalized, a time that doesn't need to abide by the terms of the contract because the contract hasn't started yet. Yes, I'm ready to be careful, but first, this week is going to require the opposite; it's going to require some danger and war—but after all that, I promise I want to be a touch careful. And maybe we can do that together."

I stopped talking, and she didn't say anything for five seconds.

"That's the end of your head letter?" she asked.

"It is," I said. "What do you think?"

"I think you sound like Thelma wants to lick Louise's pussy," she said, getting out of the Corvette. She walked by our broken parking meter, greeted her friend, and Cassidy entered the storm, surrounded by flower petals and kids. I followed, turned my face toward the sky, let some petals land on me. I had to feel the whole storm.

"Okay, danger and war this week," said Cassidy. "Then it's a touch careful from there on out. I accept those terms."

She put her hand out so we could shake on our business deal, which made me laugh.

"When," Cassidy asked, "are you gonna tell me what this Sid & Nancy thing is all about?"

"I want to tell you something about my ancestors," I said, "because they knew how to get the attention of their adversaries. Do you know how they did it? They stole. They stole from the churches trespassing in Norway. My people sacked the churches, took the money, the gold, and killed the clergy. My ancestors burned these churches to the ground. That was the only way to attract the attention of their real enemy."

"Who was that?"

"The one who never wants to be seen, like this corporate investor," I said. "The one who stays far away from the field of battle."

Meanwhile, the petals continued to rain down on our faces.

"But you take enough from the real enemy, they have to come," I said. "So we're going to kick them in their deep pockets."

ᛗ

Ah, yes. Finally. It was time.

The Ol' Sid & Nancy.

Street nobility. Filthy royals. Rulers of the gutter kingdom. Sid was known, of course, from his short time in the Sex Pistols, but it wasn't widely known that he didn't even play bass on their only studio record. He joined later. Played some shows. Died. The band made only that one album, thirty-eight minutes of music, and we're still talking about them. That was all it took for them to change the world, thirty-eight minutes.

Another important number: forty-one. We had forty-one keys to forty-one properties. And over the course of the week, we visited all forty-one, waiting for Cassidy to find out where her brother Ced's ashes were. Apparently Ced's dad moved around the Bay Area a lot, and she was still networking to track him down.

"I guess," she said, "I should be Sid Vicious. My name is Cas-*SID*-y, after all."

"I don't want to be Nancy."

"That's sexist."

Now, some etiquette: You never pulled a Sid & Nancy in normal times. No, this was a break glass in times of emergencies or witch magic—and since I intended all this as a provocation for battle, I figured, okay, let's go.

Break glass.

Raise fists.

And the Ol' Sid & Nancy was off and running. It was time for us to hit the stage, hit the town, cloud our judgment, run the numbers, buzz the tower, walk the plank. We were gonna do it fast and dirty, pure Viking madness; I could feel the adrenaline getting ready to set sail, the kind of wunjo that you got charging into violence. Channeling the Ol' Sid & Nancy required a complete disassociation from our regular code—we got into character—we changed forms—we shucked our consciences and spit them against the wall—

We were wolves.

These people were the enemy.

Making cities unaffordable, unlivable.

They were getting what they deserved.

The first empty house on our list was gonna kick off in the proper spirit of S&N, hell yes, we had a chain saw.

Where did we get a chain saw?

Tony had it stashed at the office, and I operated under one philosophy: When the universe gifted you a chain saw, you fucking chainsawed.

So that's what we did.

We chainsawed till the cows came home.

We chainsawed walls, chainsawed floors, chainsawed sinks, chainsawed tiles, chainsawed ceilings, chainsawed shelves, chainsawed cabinets, chainsawed counters, chainsawed light fixtures, chainsawed the wires in the walls, chainsawed the fuse box, chainsawed the water heater, chainsawed the guts right out of the place.

And let me tell you, if you had never chainsawed a residence before, it was war on your hands, your wrists, forearms burning. The meat of each palm buzzing, so it didn't feel good on the body, but on the inside, I enjoyed myself. Back in the day, the Vikings had something to fight for. They had land and a way of life, and they had invaders. But I had nothing. A convict fresh out. Of course I knew the right thing to do was put the chain saw down and go get a job waiting tables, though most restaurants aren't pining for a one-eyed giant slinging paella. The point was I knew that burning airplanes and chainsawing houses weren't the answers. They were just all I knew.

We blew the second house up.

We used a sledgehammer on the third.

We flooded the fourth.

We released a platoon of racoons in the fifth.

On the rest we used termites, rats, squirrels, baseball bats.

Centipedes.

Cockroaches.

Mosquitoes.

Bedbugs.

Lice.

We used fire, water.

We wheat-pasted the walls.

We filled one with wet cement.

Sometimes we looked at each other and smiled during these romantic raids. We'd say sweet things to each other. "Thanks for asking me out on a date even though I shit in that fish tank," Cassidy said to me.

We superglued the floor of an entire luxury apartment, turning it into a bourgeoise flytrap; any realtor wearing fancy shoes would stick to the floor. We used a bowling ball in one, rolling it down the hardwood floors, heaving it through windows, letting it dent every wall it wanted. We threw strikes, spares, splits. We bowled a perfect game.

We filled another with an entire dumpster of food waste, then released a festival of maggots.

We painted one place with black mold spores.

We used claw hammers.

We used an army of kittens to litter box one up.

We gave the keys of one house to a pack of junkies, told them to do their worst. We put bats in an attic. Another house had a piano in it, and I lit the instrument on fire. I actually played it while it caught, my fingers on the keys as smoke wafted from its top, and as the flames broke free from their captivity, I stood and watched the wall behind the piano break out in a rash of fire.

We used carpenter ants; we used powder-post beetles and a colony of honeybees.

We kept chainsawing.

Honestly, we chainsawed every chance we got.

I stole a moped and tore ass down the halls, squealing tires, leaving skid marks, and parked it in the living room, letting the engine chug through a whole tank of gas, pumping exhaust in the cramped space, poisoning the whole house. The drywall was a smoker's lung.

We packed the walls of one with frozen salmon.

We poured concrete down the drains of another.

We spray-painted one, and I even left my new mantra on one wall: BE FAR OUT!

We raided a gardening store and filled another with fertilizer. We packed the shit in tight.

We drove a car into the living room of another.

We, of course, kept chainsawing when the mood struck.

We chainsawed like champions.

Why? You had to give the kids what they want, had to play the classics.

I took out my phone to snap pictures. Once we finished the S&N, I'd make Tony email the whole photo series of destruction to the corporate investors. I'd razed their lands, and once I showed them the evidence, they'd come to me. That was what happened when you annihilated millions of dollars of overpriced real estate: These landlord swine come to squash the uprising.

Cassidy and I were happy to be the uprising.

"AND ARE WE MAKING GOOD DECISIONS?"

That was Python Wally talking. He wanted to know things, as he scratched at his huge beard with his bicep in the halfway house's kitchen, forearm-deep in the ol' Almighty, the squish of the ground beef as we made sure all the ingredients mixed. Each time we doctored a batch, the noises sounded barnyard to me.

Wally said it again: "And are we making good decisions?"

You bubble-wrapped demigods, you tonsil hockey matadors, you blood bank jailbirds, you pocket rockets, you taco trucks, you impulse purchases, you latchkey kids, you sagas—and could you win a fistfight with a mean-spirited parrot who spoke with a Spanish accent?

Wait.

I didn't want to answer him, but I needed to stop stalling. "I found whom I was looking for," I said.

"And they're all right?"

"I don't know yet. She's getting checked out at the hospital. Needs to detox. Needs to have her brain scanned."

"Well, that's all fantastic," Python Wally said. "I'm glad it worked out."

We were done with the mixing and were now beginning to shape the Almighty into landing strips.

"She's going to need a place to stay," I said.

"She doesn't have anyone to help her?"

Me. I was helping her. She couldn't see it, and it felt important that Wally could. "That's what I'm doing."

"I get that," he said, "but since you bunk in a halfway house, she'll likely need somebody involved who is less convict-y than you."

"Convict-y?"

"I make meatloaf and adjectives," said Python.

"She's tight with some people who live out at Slide City. I bet they'd be willing to get involved. But, well, you're not going to like this part."

Our meatloaf people movers were growing in stature—and Wally looked at me with disappointment. "How much am I not going to like this?" he asked.

"I'm in possession of the keys of a place that used to be her old place," I said.

"You're in possession?"

"Yeah."

"Of keys?"

"Uh-huh."

"Whose are they?" Wally asked.

"I worry that explanation is going to sound convict-y."

I tried explaining it as best I could, and about thirty seconds later, Python got it. Then he said to me, "I thought you were working toward joy."

"I am."

"How?"

"All this time I'm spending with Cassidy," I said.

"If you're getting sweet on her, that probably advocates for doing fewer illegal things."

"I want to take Mom Jon to the house that used to be her house," I said. "I want her to get to walk around. I want her to know that it's hers."

"It isn't."

"They basically stole her house."

"That sucks," he said, "but it's not worth you getting busted back."

"All we'd need to do—"

"I wish you knew how to take care of yourself," he said.

We padded and kneaded the teeter-totters of meat in quiet. I didn't mind Python giving me a hard time. He was right. He was giving the same advice as Cassidy—slow down, find peace and quiet, decide to live a life that wouldn't get you thrown in a cage again. I didn't know how to make him understand: This was the only way I knew how to love people.

Then Harding stormed in the kitchen. He had on another pair of immaculate Jordans, red and white. "You two," he said to us, "you're up."

"We're engaged in meatloaf production," Python said.

"We need to help someone from our class," said Harding. "We need to be the ones to listen to him. Before he's gone."

"Where's he going?" I said.

Harding told us that one of the house residents, Lopez, pissed dirty, meaning he was heading back. He'd be out of the house and back to processing within the hour. Wally shot me quite a stare, one that wondered, *Perhaps you and Lopez can cell up together if you keep stealing keys.*

Harding waved at us like an anxious third base coach coaxing a runner to move faster. "Come on. Now. You two are going to be his audience," Harding said. "You're going to take your hands out of that meat and you are going to listen, because this motherfucker was dumb enough to piss hot."

"Okay, fine, jeez," we said.

Lopez stumbled into the kitchen, pallid; he'd obviously been crying. "I can't believe I fucked my life again," he said.

Which prompted another knowing stare from Wally to moi.

Then Lopez read to us, all of us, even you:

"Before I found drugs," he said, "I came from money—came up with everything. Every opportunity. One time my family headed to an elephant sanctuary in Thailand. That's how much money we have. We go to jungles and pet elephants. I feed one watermelon, and it goes crazy for it. They have a sweet tooth, elephants. Then a few years later, I get a sweet tooth, too, for heroin, though my family and me don't know anything about that yet while we're at the elephant sanctuary. We don't know that my parents will throw me out, that I'll burn too many bridges for couch surfing, that I'll be living on the street, staying higher than giraffe pussy. One night, I'll get jumped, taking a real *beat up from the feet up*. They'll hammer me, and I'll really think my life is about to end, and in that desperation, I'll try to save my life by hitting one with an empty bottle that's on the ground next to me as I'm being kicked, and I'll rocket up and crack it right on his temple, and he'll go stiff, fall down, turn off. I'll do my time. I'll do shit in there that will plague me forever. I'll be here at the halfway house. I'll be forced to read this story to you motherfuckers, but all that bullshit hasn't happened yet. Remember that, in this story, I'm only a boy, and my family hasn't had enough of me yet, and we are in Thailand and I am feeding watermelon to an elephant. Right then, somebody who works there invites us to a separate area where one of the other elephants is going to paint a picture. 'Who is going to paint a picture?' I ask, and she says, 'The elephant,' and so because we've been teased with this unbelievable taste, we jet over to watch the show. Sure enough, there is a man standing next to an elephant, and they are in front of an easel. The man dips the brush in paint, and he holds it out to the elephant, who takes it in her trunk and starts to draw a shape, connecting lines with accuracy and nimble fucking care, and slowly I understand what she's doing: The elephant is drawing an elephant. I'm only a kid, but I remember wondering: *Who is this elephant painting? Is it a self-portrait? Is it a picture of someone the elephant loves or misses? Is it a mean mother? A careless father? Can an elephant honor the dead in ink?* After that day, I drive my parents nuts at bedtime, peppering them with these questions nonstop, and of course no one can know the truth, except that elephant. She knows, but she doesn't owe anybody an explanation. *Paint, girl.* That's what I say. Okay, so now I'm not a kid anymore in this story. Now I'm a man. Now I've killed. I'm locked up. That's when the elephant begins visiting me. I hadn't even thought of her in decades. I'd forgotten about the painting elephant until she started showing up in my dreams. I'm serious. Like every night. But she isn't interested in painting elephants anymore. All she does now, night after night, she storms into my dreams and takes that brush in her trunk, and in big letters, she paints GUILTY. I can't make her stop. I beg her. I promise I'll do whatever she wants. I'll be her slave. I'll light myself on fire. *Just please, stop. Just please, some peace. Please, elephant, don't use my tiny stable of happy childhood memories against me. Please don't devour those memories from my head like they're watermelon.* And I thought that I never wanted to see her again, and then, one night, she doesn't paint anything in my dream. Not the next night, either. She's gone again. I get what I want—what I think I want. I'm free from her. Then I go to the hole for fighting. Four months in solitary. Four inhumane months. Chained up. They drag me to the shower on a dog leash. I'm so starved for human contact that I beg the elephant to come back and visit me.

I beg her to paint GUILTY. I beg her to torture me, to make me feel. I need somebody else around, even if she is an invisible elephant. I try desperately to reach her, to conjure her, bribe her, threaten her. But I can't make her come back. I can't do anything except sit in the dark. And think. And that's the worst part, all that thinking. Our brains are janky palaces. Mine always wants me to leave, suggests to my body that I should die. So I want to die. Back in my cell, I keep a bone crusher in the toilet, a big piece of Plexiglas. If the shank doesn't kill you, the infection from the toilet will. And as much as it hurts to admit, the shank is all I want in the hole, so I can end this suffering. So I can dream again. So I can watch her trunk clutch the brush, the elephant not painting another elephant this time, and certainly not scribbling GUILTY. No, now, she simply draws a picture of a big yellow sun. And if there is a way that I can smuggle it in here and hang it on the wall in the hole, that's what I'd do, a picture of a big yellow sun, and even in the hole, I'd be warm in the light."

IT WAS WARM, and I was in the light; it was the next morning.

I felt slow, giddy. I was a jar of lukewarm bacon fat. A glob of peanut butter stuck in someone's throat. I was a terrified Alzheimer's patient who'd crashed their time machine into Walmart. I was an LSD garden party, a Russian roulette sex club. I was Invisalign to straighten a moral code.

Cassidy grabbed me in the Corvette and sped to the hospital. I didn't know what to expect seeing Mom Jon. She'd still be getting kicked in the teeth with withdrawal, but hopefully, they were keeping her comfortable, hydrated. It was brutal wherever it happened, county jail or the Ritz.

By week's end, she'd be equalizing. Then we'd know about her brain. If she was going to remember me. If she didn't, I wasn't only losing her but also any hope of getting the happy monster. I'd be losing two people. Guitars were people. I didn't know much, but I did know that.

I walked back into emergency, and the guard who had helped me first get her into the hospital stood at his post near the front door.

"How did she do getting admitted?" I asked him.

He gave me the blank stare, didn't remember me.

"That older lady," I said, doing my best not to shake him back and forth. "Talking to the hedge. Ringing any bells?"

"Do you know how many people talk to the hedges around here?" he said. "Man, those hedges know all the secrets."

"You should remember people," I said to him.

He did at least point me in the right direction of visitor check-in. I gave them Mom Jon's information, and an elderly woman helped me. She had short hair that she parted in the middle and wore big hipster glasses. "She doesn't want to see any visitors today," she said.

"Did you tell her it was me?"

"Yes."

"What did she say?"

I must've looked wounded when I asked that question, because the woman said, "I know this is hard."

I wished she weren't being so kind. It made me want to cry. "I'm going to go," I said.

"Come back tomorrow," she said. "I want to see you tomorrow." She smiled at me, this bureaucratic angel, pummeling me with compassion. I had no choice but to agree. She wasn't asking.

It was on the rarest occasions that I thought of my mother, but she buzzed through me right then. If she'd lived, I liked to believe that she would've gotten sober. Maybe we'd be friends now. Maybc we could reminisce on the night she *almost* fell off the bar in that Mexican restaurant in Phoenix; yes, it was a close call, a near miss, *almost* hitting her head, but, phew, she was fine. Though that wasn't what happened. She did fall and die. She was only on the bar doing gymnastics because she wanted a free drink, so that was the takeaway of my mother's life: She killed herself for a free drink.

But maybe she didn't and maybe she was alive and maybe she had her shit together now, and maybe she also worked at this hospital and helped people. She spent her life in service. Maybe she was as kind as this woman in front of me.

"Yes, I'll see you tomorrow," I said to her.

ᛗ

Earlier in the week, we'd moved Tony from his office to Unit 12, and before you get all hopped up on a gust of the old high and mighty, flapping insults toward me for this inhumane treatment of Tony, we were only talking about a prison sentence of a couple weeks, tops. Then he'd be free, fine. I came from a place where our incarcerations were measured in years, so I was operating under the opinion that we'd given Tony a tied-up vacation, some time to relax. Granted, the meals at the Unit 12 resort revolved around force fed shawarma (when his mouth wasn't gagged), but hey, a vacation was a vacation.

As we'd initially shuttled him in, we captured the free-range balloons, now more than half deflated, from the lobby and made Unit 12 their barn, the room full of their red and yellow glow. The air current from a cracked window made them shuffle around the living room like stoned ghosts.

Now, as we approached Unit 12, I felt a barb of wunjo, anticipating Tony emailing the pictures of the S&N to the suits. I wanted them to see my damage; I wanted to use my fists. Unit 12 wouldn't be safe for us, once the pics were emailed, so we'd make camp at Cassidy's when I wasn't at the halfway house.

Or that was the plan.

I reached for 12's front door, and there was a large manila envelope stuck to it that had my name on it, first and last. Cassidy and I stood there, staring.

"Who's that from?" asked Cassidy.

"If it's from whom I think it's from, I fucked up."

"It's from them, isn't it?"

I tore it open in the hall. It was a thick packet of pages about Unit 12, legalese sheet music, the songs of the fat cats. Privilege papers. You knew their albums even if you'd never purchased one. They brought us such hits as "Hey, Who Needs Health Insurance?" and "Rent Forever, You Rats!"

I didn't know how to read word one of this Harvard-fucked-a-Rubik's-Cube kind of fancy contract, so I handed the ribbon of bureaucracy to Cassidy, who thumbed through the first couple of pages, then said, "Well, that's fucking fascinating."

She had a beautiful smile on her face.

Green Day could write quite a catchy ballad about it.

"Do you remember the day we first met?" she said.

"It was last week."

"What was the thing I was going to say to people right before I opened the door to show them the place? Do you remember that line?"

"You were going to tell them 'Welcome home.'"

She held up the bushel of lawyer language and shook the pages at me. "Welcome home. This place is in your name now."

These fat cats, apparently, were full of surprises.

I was prepared for threats. I wouldn't have been surprised if fists or weapons had popped out of the manila envelope. It seemed reasonable to think Genghis Khan might be in there as an enforcer, a deterrent, an antidote, a skeleton key, an emissary, a confidant, a camgirl.

"Why would they do that?" I asked Cassidy.

"You're ruining the effect of my sweet fucking 'welcome home' message," said Cassidy. "But good question. Why *would* they do that?"

She had magic sailing in her bloodstream. "I'm sorry to ruin your effect," I said.

"Let's try it again," she said, "and 'welcome home' and just say thanks."

I pinned her to the outside of Unit 12, and we were ready to go right there. I was on her neck, kissing, biting softly, biting a bit harder, huffing like a wolf in her ear. She had her hand on my throat.

I knew that they were setting me up for something, but I'd worry about that later. For now, we'd fall into this new home, and we'd fall into a slow fuck, and we'd spend the afternoon naked and napping. Then we'd deal with their treacherous paperwork.

Wait.

Shit.

Tony was inside. If they had been here, they most likely found him, let him go. All my leverage would be gone.

"Hold on," I said to Cassidy, and threw the front door open, and because we'd kept the curtains drawn for obvious Tony-storage reasons, I turned on the lights. Surprisingly, he was still there, tied to his chair. Just like we'd left him.

That was a true statement.

But there was also a saber sticking out of his chest, one of those vintage swords from the Napoleonic Wars with the curved blade.

That was not good. Certainly, it wasn't good for dead Tony. It also killed the mood between Cassidy and me. In addition to that, they were leaving me quite a business card. *Yeah*, their card read, *we're fat cats, but we're also murderers.*

Cassidy and I walked over and stood in front of him, marveling. We let some time pass. It was the kind of quiet that allowed you to be masochistically openhearted. And perhaps, under normal conditions, I might use such solitude, such inspiration, to throat a new melody or write a new run up the happy monster's strings. Aggressive and sludgy. Mean and fast and defiant.

Instead, and I'm aping off Op Ivy here, this was the moment when I knew that I knew nothing.

"That's a sword," I said.

"It sure is."

"In his chest."

"Congratulations," Cassidy said, "you're the proud owner of a condo and a dead guy."

M

You mercy kill, you meat substitute, you sex robot—

We were, understandably, distracted by the dead guy. Cassidy and I stood in Unit 12, in front of Tony, the eyebrow-shaving snake, admiring the sword jutting from his chest that, from profile, turned Tony into the shape of a lowercase *r*.

As you could imagine, simply metabolizing the grisly details of Tony's murder courted the majority of our attention. We were not very attuned to our environment or circumstances, save the center of the frame, this guy Tony, stabbed in the heart with a sword.

Since we were a touch, uh, distracted, we didn't peep the note sitting on the kitchen counter, where, earlier, she'd kept her tray of semifrozen shrimp, those little Popsicles of the ocean that meant so much to me.

Now, in their place, was a single typed page, three lines:

A gift.
A debt.
We'll be in touch.

"So the real estate assholes gave you this place?" Cassidy asked.

"Yes."

"Meaning Tony's partners?"

"Right."

"So his bosses planted a saber in his chest?" she said.

"That's what I'm assuming."

"If the gift from their note is the condo, what's the debt?"

"From their perspective, it's probably all the property damage we caused."

"Or Tony's body could be the debt."

"No," I said, "because we're sniffing around, they're taking out the trash. Tony knows too much."

"I agree that the property damage is a debt that matters later," Cassidy said, "but our immediate debt is a dead body in a place that you now own."

"Yeah, we have to get Tony out of here," I said. "For all we know, the cops are on their way."

"Sorry, but I'm all out of plans that revolve around getting a sword-murdered guy out of your house," she said.

"This is—at first—going to sound excessive," I said, "but let me get to the end before you call me a psycho."

"An excessive psycho?"

"It could go either way."

"I can't tell if this is turning me on," Cassidy said.

"We drive him out in the 'Vette on Highway 1, those crazy curves by the ocean. We plop him into the driver's seat and steer the car into the Pacific."

"It's a shame to lose the 'Vette."

"It's a bigger shame to go to prison."

"I have some questions," she said. "So in the reality of this hypothetical suicide, Tony stabbed himself in the chest with a sword and went for a drive?"

"Yeah, maybe driving was his favorite thing, so he wanted to die doing something he dug, speeding on the open road."

"But you said the car crashes into the ocean."

"Maybe he liked driving and swimming," I said.

"Not your best work," she said.

"Or we take him back to his office. 'Real Estate Parasite Prick Kills Himself at His Desk.' Half the people who read the headline will give it a standing ovation."

"That's better," said Cassidy.

M

We got extra creative in our transport. Here was when we used almost all the half-filled red balloons as a kind of camouflage. We loaded Tony into a golf bag and put him in the center of a luggage rack, stacked other suitcases around, and tied those balloons to handles. It was hard to tell what was going on behind that red protection. Then we loaded him into the car and carried the golf bag into his office.

All his fish had died. It smelled like hell in there.

"We forgot to feed the fish," Cassidy said, and she started crying. She walked over to the tank and put her hand up near the surface, where their bodies all floated. “I’m sorry,” she said to them. “It’s not your fault. It’s mine.”

I came and stood next to her. It surprised me to see her so upset about their demise. I didn’t track their significance to her. I wanted to ask her about that, and maybe I would later. For now, all she needed from me was my understanding, even if I didn’t.

“I should’ve remembered to feed them, too,” I said.

“What do you think is going to happen to us?” Cassidy asked, using her finger to steer one of the dead fish around the surface, like it had driven Tony’s ’Vette off Highway 1 and now bobbed in the ocean.

“What do you mean?”

She piloted the dead fish, and it crashed into the other floating bodies. “Do you think we’ll ever learn to be a touch careful?”

“I don’t know,” I said, but here’s what I should’ve said: *Careful can’t feel like a consolation prize. Careful needs to feel like a reward. And that’s what I want to learn, Cassidy. Can I ever find the treasure of peace?*

“You should know,” she said.

Fresh out of that stretch, all those years in Quentin, the constant guard, the eyes in the back of your head, the get-ready right under the surface all the time, day and night. Every noise was a wolf sneaking close. That wilderness was nonstop war. And I didn’t know how to turn those instincts off so fast. It was like I had weapons glued to my hands, swords or axes stuck to my limbs, and I couldn’t remember how to put them down. Was it possible to live a careful life with axes for hands?

“I’m trying to know,” I said to Cassidy. “I think it has something to do with finding my purpose.”

“It has more to do with you not committing crimes.”

"And the purpose thing, too," I said.

"I don't think we can," she said. "I think the two of us are dead fish, too."

She pulled her finger from the tank and wiped the dead fish germs on my jeans. That must be what a loving marriage looks like. You could wipe whatever you wanted on somebody else's pants.

"I don't think you're a dead fish, Cassidy."

"Flirt."

And that made me feel a breeze of joy.

And that made me lean over and kiss Cassidy next to the rancid fish tank.

"You're not a dead fish, either," she said to me.

We propped Tony up behind his desk, and now we needed to slide the sword back into his chest. We'd removed it for ease of transport and then rubbed the handle clean of fingerprints.

"Do you want to do the honors?" I asked Cassidy.

"Do I want to stab him with a saber?" she said. "Of course I want to stab him with a saber!"

"You can't stab him," I said. "You need to gently put it back in the existing gash."

"That's not as fun."

"Maybe you can pretend that you're stabbing him in slow motion," I said, hoping she'd hear the romance in the suggestion. I was meeting her in the stabbing middle, and it didn't get more romantic than that.

Cassidy laughed. "A slow-motion stab?"

She'd forgotten how upset she was about the fish, which was what I wanted. Then she really went for the Oscar, in her performance of Slow-Motion Stab. She raised the sword above her head at quarter speed and slowed her speech to droning moans. "Eyebrow payback!"

Then, like a proper warrior, Cassidy slid the sword right into the heart of her enemy, raised her hands, still slowly, in victory. We stood in front of him, dead at his desk with a saber in his chest, the room reeking of rotting fish.

"Do you want to say anything about him?" I asked her.

She thought for a minute. "I should've shaved his eyebrows."

"We can do it now, if you want."

"Nah, this way I have the high road," said Cassidy.

She was able to keep it together for about two seconds before she started laughing, this time at the idea that she and I were on the high road. People like us weren't allowed in rarefied air. We got the gruel, the grease, the moonshine, the swing shift, the bad break, the black lung, the pill problem, the fine print, the predatory loans. Then she spoke right to dead Tony: "Do you hear me? I'm way up on the high road, and you're dead all the way down there."

It didn't seem like she wanted me to say anything, so I shut up. There were different kinds of quiet in this life: This one was peculiar, mainly due to the fact that the whole room smelled like low tide, salty rot, and there was Tony minding his own business at his desk, and the two of us were together, and, somehow, I was having the best time on our careless quest.

Finally, she said, "I found out where he has Ced's ashes."

"Then let's go get your brother."

"I don't know if I can see his dad without losing my shit," she said. "Can you get my brother for me?"

ABOUT TWO IN THE AFTERNOON of a proper seventy-degree day, I knocked on the door of a run-down house in East Oakland. It was a ranch-style place that hadn't been doted on in a long time. The front yard was fenced-in concrete. There was a plane in the sky, one of those that had an advertising tail, an aerial banner, and this one said: SAVE THE BAY FROM TECH BROS.

I was excited to help Cassidy, who waited out in the 'Vette. I wanted to give her a gift, my gift, the gentle touch of a punk rock Viking. Here was what I couldn't make Python Wally understand: Helping Cassidy felt like purpose to me, a calling. And there were many worse ways to spend a life than helping people.

A bald man, one whom Cassidy called Daddy Nightmares, answered the door. Before I saw his body, I saw the camera he held, black and bulky. It rested on his shoulder, and he blocked the doorway with that beast of a camera.

"An uninvited guest!" he said, ecstatic. "That's just what this episode needs. And your style! That mohawk! The casting department outdid themselves this time!"

"You know Cassidy, right?" I asked.

"This doesn't have to be a cameo for you," he said. Daddy Nightmares had a big spiderweb tattoo on his skull, was out of shape, looked like he wore his little brother's shirt, water-ballooning it to such capacity that I could see his chest hair through it. "Give a lively performance," he said, "and this could be a recurring role."

"You're the father of her brother Ced?"

"My friend, this isn't how you introduce yourself to the audience. At all. You're not reeling them in. Start with a joke. Make them laugh. A little raunchy? A dash theatrical? It's all gold. Give 'em the giggles. Camaraderie, baby! Once the audience is on your side, they'll follow you anywhere."

"I'm here for Ced's ashes."

"Do you know what a joke is?"

"Get the ashes."

"Fine. Jokes aren't your thing," he said. "I get it. We can't all be natural comedians. But we can work on it. I can school you in the art of hilarity. Here. I'll show you how it's done. This one's an oldie but a goodie: When is it okay to beat up a dwarf?"

He turned the camera around, so it framed his face, and talked right at the lens: "Do you have any guesses at home?"

He pointed it back at me and asked, "So what's the answer?"

I'd had enough of his mouth, and I put a single jab in his solar plexus, then two-hand pushed him in the chest; he fell backward, couldn't breathe. I had a habit of storming into people's houses these days, but only if you were an ash-stealing asshole or two deranged brothers holding Mom Jon hostage in a dark house surrounded by a thicket of wind turbines.

What, you don't believe me?

What, you don't think I can be a team player?

I can prove it. In Quentin, my first cellie was a small man, but hard. Marine Corps. During the first Gulf War, he'd done urban patrol in Baghdad. Once his active service was over, he came home. Two months later, he murdered his upstairs neighbor for walking too loud. Right as I'd entered his cell for the first time, he told me that there were two rules in his house. Rules weren't my favorite things, but I was going to hear him out.

"You have to piss sitting down," he said. "This is a splash-free zone."

That wasn't what I was expecting to hear from him, and if he wanted to take pride in where he lived, I had no problem with that. "This is your spot," I said, "so I'll do it. What's the other rule?"

"Do you have a release date?"

"Yes."

"So you're getting out of here."

"Yes."

"I'm not," he said, "so I don't ever want to hear you fucking gripe about how hard your time is. You get to leave. So you shut the fuck up. Do you understand me?"

He'd already survived one scheduled death penalty. He'd even read about his own murder in the newspaper, which said he'd die by lethal injection the next day, till the governor called it off at the last minute. Clemency, maybe. Or the State of California couldn't even kill right. The man had the article about his execution on the wall of the cell, like you'd frame a diploma or a wedding photo. But not in here, no. In this madhouse you commemorated the day of your death even as you went on living. His favorite part of the story was that before his stay was granted, he'd already gorged on his last supper: a root beer float and extra-greasy onion rings, enough ketchup to re-create a crime scene. Me, I always imagined what it must be like to be the chef preparing these final meals. You controlled the flavors that would linger in the mouth as someone left this world for good. You were an angel with a spatula, and as the poisons dripped into their bodies and as those corruptions shut off their hearts, at least they had happy bellies bulging with comfort food.

Now, once he finished telling me the rules, I walked over to the toilet, dropped my pants, sat, pissed. “It certainly looks like I’m assimilating,” I said.

See? Never let it be said that I couldn’t abide by the customs of a new clan.

Some people’s homes deserved to be treated with respect and some didn’t.

Back to East Oakland, back to the aftermath of a body jab and a two-hand shove, back to the bald man called Daddy Nightmares sprawled on the floor, on his ass, righting his bulky camera so it framed me, and once he could fill his lungs again, he said, “Fantastic! An action sequence! If you can’t make them laugh, make their armpits sweat with high-stakes violence. Let them wonder if we’re gonna get out of this alive.”

I entered his house and shut the door behind me. Locked it. “Put the camera down, go get Ced’s ashes,” I said, “or I’m going to separate your shoulders.”

He pointed the camera at his face once more, said to the lens, “It’s okay to beat up a dwarf when he’s standing crotch-tall next to your girlfriend, and he tells her that her hair smells delicious.”

I moved toward him, grabbed at the camera, broke it on the ground. I put a knee on his throat and sat on him for a quick chat. Immediately, his face found another camera, this one a small device mounted on the ceiling. He talked into it: “A wide shot is probably better anyway.”

“Are people seeing this live right now?” I asked.

"No. My subscribers will watch today tomorrow," he said. "They are always seeing yesterday. Today I live, and tomorrow I'm content."

I slapped him across the face.

"What are you doing here?" I said. "What are you filming?"

I smacked him another time. This second blow was wildly unnecessary, but I found him to be an annoying person—and that was before factoring in him ransoming the ashes.

"Now that you've broken into my house," he screamed to the camera on the ceiling, "this must be the season finale."

"Are you ready to get me the ashes, or should I get a jump on separating shoulder number one?"

He smiled at me. "Yes, you're here to help with the finale. So of course I'll help you, too. Let's go get those ashes. Let's all go together," and he said the last line with a kind of Mr. Rogers singsong toward the camera.

I got off him, and he popped up.

"Yes, let's venture and get you those ashes," he said. "I know right where they are. Sort of. They're in one of my boxes. Back here."

I followed him down the hall to the end of it . . .

. . . where there were two bedrooms.

One of them had nothing in it but stacked boxes, save for one detail mounted up on the ceiling. Another camera.

"Ced's in one of these," he said, kicking a box. "He's content, too."

"You're a piece of shit," I said.

"That's true," he said.

"I'm not here to help you."

"Of course you are," he said, and plucked down one of the top boxes.

"Why didn't you just let Cassidy have the ashes?" I asked.

He began to inspect the first box. "This one's junk." He pulled out an old broken baseball trophy. "I coulda been a contendah," he said, winking at the camera, then lowered his voice to me, saying, "Those kinds of callbacks are pure nostalgia bait for the audience."

He stashed that box back and got down another. He pulled out heaps of paper.

"They make us math!" he said to me. "This one's IRS bullshit." Then to the camera: "Kids, pay your taxes! We all think we won't get caught cheating, and we all do. Just pay the fascists. It's not worth the hassle or the jail time."

He slammed that box back and got another one. Once he opened it, he took a moment, collecting himself before saying to the camera and me in a choked-up way, "This box is a biopic," he said. "Wedding pictures. Divorce papers. A whole arc."

He held each up separately.

The wedding picture was old. He was in it, looking so normal, like there was an entire mind in his head, while the spiderwebbed man I now watched rummaging through these boxes hadn't had a whole brain in a long time.

Was that Cassidy's mother in the picture?

"You looked so normal," I said to him.

"I gave that up," he said. "The last thing you want in this business is to be typecast. Show range. Act, sing, dance. Be a triple threat."

Then he showed the divorce papers, made a face like they stunk of bungled promises. "I was having a pretty good life until I got served with these. Then it all fell apart. Drugs, sure. But it was the gambling that really fucked me up. I've got nothing left. I'm a mannequin, a frame and some shame. And that's no way to live. So I'm going to learn how to live on a server farm. I'm going to wiggle through Wi-Fi and entertain. I'll move like digital wind. And wind lives forever."

He stored that box again and got another, rummaged around in it. "This one's old comics. These aren't content. These are art. Content is just ordered off the McDonald's menu. I want a number one. Can you whip me up a number four? Content doesn't have to taste good. We just need something to eat."

He ripped open another box and said, "Voilà! The man of the hour," and he pulled out an urn. He thrust it toward the camera like a prospector might do with a gold nugget. "My son was a good boy," he said, and started crying.

"Is that real, or are you doing it for the show?"

"Yes," he said, "that's what I'm doing."

"Which?"

"Yes," he said again, holding the urn out to me.

It wasn't fancy, a squat black cylinder. Looked like an ice bucket from a motel. But you could keep your meaningful possessions wherever you wanted, even in the songs you wrote.

"Go give him to Cassidy," he said, shaking the urn. "Make her happy and break my heart."

I didn't take the urn yet. "Break your heart? You kept him in a cardboard box. You didn't even know which one he was in."

"The grieving process is cubism," he said. "You can't judge another person's grief with an art history degree."

"You're so full of shit," I said.

"You should be making your own show, too. We're all auditioning for what comes next with the new regime." He used his fingers to crawl like an insect on his skull's spiderweb tattoo. "We had so much fun ending our world, and now it's time for some new programming. AI will be royalty."

I took the urn from him. It felt alive with a subtle current. It was a man named Ced. And he sat in my hand in an urn in a room in a house on a planet.

I was meeting Cassidy's brother for the first time. "Pleasure to meet you," I said to Ced.

"That will get everyone to turn on the waterworks," Daddy Nightmares said. "You're a natural at this. We'll make the Oscars cum so hard!"

"Before I go," I said, "why'd you do it? Why'd you try to make a buck off your kid's ashes?"

"You break into my house and steal my son," he said, "and I'm the bad guy?"

"You hurt Cassidy, and I'm starting to care about her very much. So yes, at least to me, you're the bad guy."

"You're the best scene partner I've had in a very long time," he said. "We should both put this on our reels."

"What are you fucking talking about?"

"AI overlords. We can't stop trying to replace ourselves. We're obsessed with obsolescence. We're dinosaurs building the asteroid that will kill us all. You'll never win a fight with an asteroid. So we'll be living in their world. And they'll only keep the ones of us who are useful to them, and what can we really offer? They're better than us in every way. All we can be is their entertainment. We can be their court jesters and that's it. So that's what I'm doing. I'm auditioning for our AI asteroid. I'll be their wind."

"You haven't answered my question. Why did you try to sell Ced's ashes?"

"The answer is *always* money," he said. "I was in a hole. I would've sold anything. I'm the piece of shit who tried to sell his dead son to pay a debt."

"I'm leaving now," I said.

"Resolution," he said. "The hero gets what he wants. The audience is satisfied with the dramatic resolution. A happy ending!"

He was right. This was a happy ending. Cassidy would be reunited with her brother, and there were still hours left in the afternoon before I needed to be back at the halfway house. Maybe we could all walk on the beach together. Maybe Cassidy, inspired by the ashes' presence, would want to tell old stories of her and Ced, trek memory lane for stories. I could learn more about their childhoods, hear their inside jokes, the load-bearing traumas, the broken bones of a broken home. I could nod along to all these meaningful vignettes and appreciate the naked access to someone's past.

Maybe we could—

But then Daddy Nightmares's chest exploded.

THE SHOT CAME FROM BEHIND ME, whistled by my body. A blossoming understanding of the wreck, as the bald man's eyes saw the blood. Cassidy stood in the doorway, her gun still pointing at him.

He held his hands to his chest, and his eyes bulged. His body was forgetting how to live. Or his body knew that he was losing things that it needed to live. Either way, he wouldn't have what it took to be here much longer.

"Why did you do that?" I said to her. "He already gave me the ashes!"

"He did more."

"What?"

"He did more. To my brother and me."

"Cassidy," I said, "we'll do life for this."

He still wasn't dead, gazing at us with wonder and panic, and he smacked his lips, looking for saliva. He wanted to say something. He wanted us to know a final message. He'd never be wind, never try his luck as an AI court jester. He was another man with a hole in his chest. He smacked his lips a couple more times and tried to talk, and nothing came out.

"No, I already got life, just now," she said to me. "I got life when I pulled the trigger. I got mine back."

She was in the zip ties of shock. Her face had no expression. Her mouth moved, but the rest of her body could've been in suspended animation, submerged in hypnosis, a coffin carved out of a glacier. Again, he smacked his lips a couple more times and tried to talk, and nothing came out.

I grabbed her by the wrist, hard, wanting to lead her out, toss her in the car, and get out of there as fast as we could. But she shook me off, stepped back, put her hands up between us. Again, he smacked his lips a couple more times and tried to talk, and nothing came out.

"He did more so I did more. That's fair," she said to me. "That's the only thing I know: This is fair."

He finally died, hands slowly falling from his bloody chest and resting on his belly. His head lolled forward, showing us the whole spiderweb on his head, then his throat emitted a hissing noise that was unlike anything I'd ever heard before. A snake playing a sax solo. We both stood for a minute, watching his newly dead body, sprawled right in front of all his cardboard boxes.

He finally stopped hissing his song.

Then Cassidy said to me, "Now it's time for you to go."

I stared.

"You didn't do this," she said. "I did. I want you to get away. You're not going back to prison. So you're leaving. So we are only going to know each other for another thirty seconds, and I know what I want to do with that time."

She let the gun fall to the floor, and she tumbled into my arms. We clasped our hands and danced, circled slowly, in this room with the cardboard boxes and the ashes and the body. In this room that only had thirty seconds left.

"I bet we could have been happy together," she said. "What do you think?"

"We would have had a blast."

"What kind of life would we have had?"

"No," I said, "I don't want to think about that."

"Why not?"

"I fucking can't."

"Tell me one thing," Cassidy said to me. "Tell me one thing from our fake future."

It was my chest's turn to explode.

"I would've taken you to Norway," I said. "I would've shown you the world that made me."

"I bet we would've gotten a dog. A big, hairy, floppy-eared dog. And something tells me that I would've learned to knit," said Cassidy

I gave her a big kiss, urgent and limitless. This was a kiss that knew everything we'd miss.

"Slip out the alley," she said. "You have to find your own way home."

I wanted to tell her how tired I was of that, finding my way home alone. I wanted to build something, wanted family.

"I have to stay," she said.

"Why?"

"That would've been a great future for us," she said, "but this dance will have to do."

"Why do you have to stay?" I asked.

"You don't have to understand," she said, sounding like Harding's writing advice: *Write what you know—but never write what you un-*

derstand. "You have to be out of here once the thirty seconds is up, so let's dance."

You're a person and she's a person and I am, and we were all in this room together, a boxed-up life, a closing-down future, and I'd likely never see her again, and I thought of my old cellie Denis, who went blind right in front of me. I had a few seconds left, and this made her even more gorgeous. And that had joy in it. A frantic joy, off its meds. They say you get euphoric before you drown, and that was the kind of wunjo I experienced right then with Cassidy. We could've had a good life; we were telling the truth about that. But sometimes you only got a thirty-second dance with somebody.

"I'm a big hypocrite," she said to me, now resting her head on my chest. "I gave you the business about being a touch careful, and then I went and shot a guy."

We wore those last thirty seconds like they were diamonds.

YOU ENDORPHIN CATHEDRAL, you lederhosen warhorse, you raggedy showboat, you castrated road rage, you ride-or-die hex, let's exchange pleasantries, greet each other with a kiss on the lips—and do you know the name of that sea creature who rubs its tail along ribbons of sea glass, like a bow across a cello's strings, and the music electrifies the water with song?

Wait.

Where were we?

Right.

I snuck from East Oakland, staying in the alleys mostly, onto BART, and now I was back at the halfway house, trying to play it cool, lie low, act natural, but my guts felt filled with Tony's dead fish.

Harding and I were scheduled to have our first one-on-one to talk about the piece I had to write for his class, and a half hour later we met in the conference room, flush with all the motivational posters heaving emo propaganda from the walls. I chose a seat near my favorite—the BE FAR OUT! was interstellar inspiration—and Harding said to me, "And you want to write about losing your eye?"

I had thought I did. *Had* thought I finally wanted to look in that dead socket and seek the truth. But now I wasn't so sure. If there was anything scarier than the truth, I'd never met it.

Now I might want to write about Cassidy.

But maybe that wasn't right: If Harding's rule for writing was to *write what you know—but never write what you understand*, that eliminated Cassidy. I completely got why she did it. I just wished she hadn't, wished she didn't shrink our future to a thirty-second dance. Like the BE FAR OUT! poster, I wanted a galaxy with her. A humongous junkyard made of space dust and gas and billions of stars, flush with solar systems, packed with time and gravity, and the two of us could soar anywhere we wanted.

We were being far fucking out, and we were together. Instead, I knew her for a week, which wasn't a galaxy at all. It was a black hole, a famished monster that gobbled our future.

It wasn't my mother's accidental death, but Cassidy left me, too.

It wasn't my father's suicide, but Cassidy left me, too.

It wasn't Rebecca's cancer, but Cassidy let me, too.

It wasn't the ballistic missiles in Mom Jon's brain, blowtorching her memories to negative space, but Cassidy left me, too.

I was the person you left behind. I was sick of OD'ing on all this despair, and suddenly, I knew I couldn't write about my eye *or* Cassidy.

"I want to write about joy," I said to Harding.

"You said you wanted to write about your eye. What changed?"

"Joy," I said to him, "that's the thing. I need to understand it. I have a new theory, Harding. It came to me the other day in the sky."

"In the sky?"

"It's an expression," I said.

"Is it?"

"Here is my new theory: Joy is gasoline. It's fuel and it's toxic. Your joy can kill you. That's something that I thought about the other day in the sky."

"Which is an expression," he said.

"It's catching on," I said. "I want joy to gas me up, not destroy me."

"So write about it then."

"But I don't want to write stories. I want to write songs."

"So write songs."

"I can do that?"

"How the hell do I know?" Harding asked. "You probably won't know if you can write a song about joy until you do it."

But I already knew. Somehow, some way, I was going to scribble punk rock that was joy and joy and joy . . .

ᛗ

I didn't forage for even a wink of sleep that night.

My skull was covered in a fun-house lacquer.

My brain was soaked with peculiar soup.

And memories were scratched records that disappointed you every time you played them, so why couldn't we stay away, and why couldn't we save ourselves?

Wait. Give me a sec.

There.

Between Ced's ashes and Cassidy, I never made it to the hospital yesterday to check on Mom Jon, so after breakfast, I headed straight over and ambushed the information desk where I had met the older volunteer two days back. She was there again, to my relief, smiling in her huge hipster eyeglasses.

Nearby, there was an old man in a wheelchair in the throes of a seizure, nurses rushing to wheel him back to the white coats. Seconds later, a young woman came by on what looked like a Zamboni doting on the ice of a hockey rink, but it only buffed the floor in the hospital, making the white tiles into rows of bleached teeth. I had been in Quentin with a man who got a DUI on a Zamboni, swerving slowly and colliding with a wall. After the impact, when they tried to muscle him off the beast, he belligerently jabbed somebody who fell and smashed their face on the ice, died from a brain bleed. I didn't pity most convicts but always felt for him: One minute you were happy-go-lucky wasted, traveling two miles an hour tending to a rink, probably whistling, cheerful and tanked; it seemed impossible that anything could rupture your peace, and then you blinked your peepers and had to soldier in a prison gang.

Now, my friend at the hospital information desk and I watched the aftermath of the seizing man in the wheelchair, and the Zamboni hummed off in a different direction, and it was time for the woman to be disappointed in me. "You're late," she judged.

"It's not even ten in the morning."

"You were supposed to be here yesterday," she said, and reached for the phone. "Let's check and see how she's doing."

"No. Wait," I said to her. "I don't know if I want you to call yet."

"Why?"

"I don't know if I can hear that she doesn't want to see me."

"We can wait," she said.

"Thanks."

"You know, it's not personal. Anything she says has nothing to do with you. She's kicking drugs, and that's an out-of-body experience where you give birth to another version of yourself."

I didn't expect to hear that kind of poetry at the information desk, and I had a huff of wunjo. It was better to know. I should know. "Okay," I said, after a deep breath, "let's make the call."

"We don't have to yet. You can watch me work."

"Okay," I said, "let's wait."

The volunteer leaned in closer and whispered, "Watching me work is more fun than it sounds. Sometimes I give people the wrong directions on purpose. Then I watch them wander the halls."

Sometimes I give people the wrong directions.

Those were lyrics to a song that needed to be written. I couldn't do it right now.

Do you have the time?

It was going to be awful to find out Mom Jon didn't know me, but it was better to know than to spend every day wondering if I was missing time with her, time that we could've been together, the two us, two people who knew the whole story. Two people who could tell you every last detail of the other's life.

"Okay," I said, "let's find out."

Sometimes I give people the wrong directions.

Then the volunteer picked up the phone and dialed. A moment later she said a few words about me and was put on hold. We waited, while she clung to the phone and I clung to flimsy hope. Then she hung up and said, "She'll see you."

ᛗ

I stoner-slunk down the first-floor hall. At the elevator bank, I regarded the shut doors like a herd of elephants, so I stood back and admired them in their natural habitat. Finally, I tiptoed close and stepped into an elevator, though it was the last place I wanted to be, in an elephant's metal belly, and I let the doors shut and didn't push a button indicating a new floor, and I was alone in there, and I couldn't get my finger to press any of the buttons, an impossible feat, my finger on strike.

And I stood there a few seconds until the doors opened back up again, and a crush of nurses hopped in with me, and now, I had no choice, had to travel into the sky, to the sixth floor. Arriving, I stepped out and inched down the hall, watching the numbers of the rooms crawling up. Here was her room; the door was closed.

The way it worked was that we used our hands to open doors. Then we pushed them wide and walked through their frames. Going into rooms wasn't hard. Not typically. But going into this one felt impossible.

I inched the door slowly open so I didn't disturb her in case she slept, in case she dreamed, and who knew, maybe she dreamed that the two of us were together, that we were doing something silly like bowling, yes, went to the most run-down alley we could find, yes, we conjured Melvins on the old jukebox like it was a rock and roll Ouija board, yes, rented cheap, stinky shoes and rolled balls down dull lanes, got lucky every once in a while and accidentally picked up a spare, but mostly, we threw gutter balls, not that we cared, the point wasn't the pins, the tally, the count, the coins, the casualties, the quagmire, the triage, the spilled beans, the lost puppies, no, the point was that we were together—together!—in a run-down bowling alley tossing gutter balls and marveling at our happy lives.

Or she was going to wake up, look me in my one good eye, and ask, "Who are you?"

The climate of her room was cleaning products. Mom Jon was out cold, hooked to an IV and a couple other squat boxes that looked like droids, which reminded me of a guy in Quentin who once said to me, "I should've killed myself four years ago after R2-D2 handed me a beer." He'd meant that literally, had been at a ritzy party where there was a droid handing out drinks, and he had too many cold ones from the robot and lost his temper and stabbed a bragging millionaire in the thigh with a fork. That was his nickname in the joint, Fork. Most people got a prison nickname and most didn't like them and that didn't matter. Once you were Fork, you were Fork.

When I asked why he did it, Fork said, "The prick wouldn't stop talking about his yacht."

Unfortunately, the bacteria on Fork's silverware wreaked havoc in the rich guy's leg, and they had to amputate it. That fork cost Fork five years in prison on an attempted murder charge. If you could afford droids, you had a pit bull lawyer on retainer. People like Fork and me got semi-alcoholic bottom-feeders as public defenders.

I was all in favor of stabbing millionaires, and he and I got along great. Fork had to gang up to stay alive inside, told me he'd cover up all his jailhouse tattoos once he got out: "I'm not a hateful person," Fork said, "just don't want to get murdered in here." He said he'd bury all their ink under happy tattoos on his first day outside. Flowers. I didn't have the heart to tell him he'd only be able to cover them up with black ink, and black flowers would look basically like shamrocks, and in Quentin, a shamrock was an Aryan tattoo. You couldn't get away from prison, even once you left.

Now, in her hospital room, I didn't want to wake Mom Jon up, so I just stood and studied. Her face was the color of cold oatmeal. At least she didn't have a roommate, save for the TV mounted on the wall, *Dirty Dancing* playing on mute. The only music was her heartbeat blaring from one droid. The beeps sounded like her body worked hard even while sleeping, the gauntlet of withdrawal testing everything she was made of.

I stood at the foot of her bed. Her mouth hung open, head tilted to the side. It looked like an uncomfortable angle, so I carefully repositioned her head on the pillow. She didn't stir. Her mouth stayed open.

I sat down on the bed next to her. Out her tinted window, there was a flagpole flying nothing, just a big cocktail stick, waiting to pick the teeth of a giant.

"It's me," I finally said to her. "I'm with you again."

On the front of her hospital gown, there was a gray stain. It was symmetrical in pattern, looked like a Rorschach inkblot, though maybe everything in the world was a Rorschach test. We all saw the same things, and we all saw different things. Right now, looking at that stain, I saw a storm cloud with lightning inside.

What did you see? What did her stain paint on the cave wall in your skull?

There was an untouched tray of food on a cart next to her bed and a big carafe of water. I dipped a paper napkin into it and then placed the wet napkin on the gown's Rorschach stain. I rubbed it back and forth gently, until the storm cloud turned into a train, a locomotive barreling too fast to handle even the slightest curve in the track. The only way to go on at this speed was to crash.

"I want to tell you something," I said to her. "I'm bunking in a halfway house, and one of the mandatory activities is a writing course. A way for us to get out our feelings so we don't go back inside. Harding teaches the classes, and I told him I wanted to write about losing my eye in Quentin. I really thought I wanted to understand that moment. But now, I don't want . . ."

I dipped a dry corner of the napkin into the carafe, going back to work on her gown.

I said, "I don't want to do it anymore. I'm not giving another thought to what has already ruined my life once. It already broke a bunch of yesterdays. Why would I let it kill today or tomorrow, too?"

It wasn't even her gown; she didn't own it. She'd be stripped out of it, and the rag would be bleached to threads before the morning rounds. And yet I couldn't care about that. There was only the fact that she wore it right this second, and she should have clean clothes.

She was still out cold, but nothing was going to stop me.

"I don't want any more wrecked days, Mom Jon," I said to her. "A friend suggested a careful life, and maybe I should try it."

The stain was gone, or so it looked like to me. We'd have to wait. It was nearly impossible to tell if that was the truth till the fabric dried. That was the only way to tell if the colors matched. I brought my hands up and rubbed my eye. It was time to leave. Come back tomorrow.

That was when I heard her parched voice asking, "Will you do me a favor?" and she pointed at the TV.

"What do you need?" I said.

Still pointing: "Turn it up. This is my favorite part."

We picked up the action right on the big dance number at the end, that horrid "(I've Had) the Time of My Life" song filling the space that seconds ago was only the sounds of her droid and heartbeat. Then Mom Jon started singing, too, and I wondered: How could she remember some dumb film from the '80s, and I was erased from her memory? Why would her brain be so cruel? She remembered every word, smiling in her hospital bed, and it was beautiful and awful and beautiful and awful.

"You should sing, too," she said.

I didn't know all the words, but I tried. I, at least, could fumble through the chorus with her, singing a wonderfully shitty pop song with a woman I loved, one who might never remember me. You could sing *the time of your life* while having the time of your life, and it could still break your heart.

Once the song ended, she asked me, "Will you do me another favor?"

Maybe she needed a sip of water or help into the bathroom, or wanted me to get somebody who worked here. Maybe she was hungry or needed to gobble some meds to help her recover. But she wasn't interested in any of that. Instead, she said to me, "Would you get me out of here?"

Did you hear that? She wanted to leave with me.

Our dreams could seem so real, we really believed we were alive.

I fished an empty wheelchair from the hall and loaded her in, had no idea if she was allowed to leave or not, and I didn't want to ask permission. This was a quest, after all. We were fleeing the bad castle of a fuming ruler. We raced out of a dark forest before it smothered us with decay. I had no idea if helping her leave was even the right thing to do. I was the one who had dropped her off here five days ago, thinking it was the move.

No such practical questions could get to me right then, because I was with Mom Jon. I pushed her down the hall, down the elevator, toward my friend, the volunteer at the information counter, who I expected would want to help in our escape. I imagined her saying to us as we rushed by, *Don't worry, I got you. I love sending people in the wrong direction, remember?*

But when we neared her station, her eyes were glued to her laptop, ogling the news. A man had been brutally gunned down in his home in

East Oakland. Another man was found stabbed to death with a saber at his place of employment in the Sunset District. The building had been burned, and arson was the chief suspicion. Authorities also believed that there was a connection between the two murders, and they were looking for a suspect. They put a picture on the screen, Cassidy. Subject was at large.

I guess she couldn't do it, couldn't sit at that house waiting for the cops, a life sentence. Maybe she hopped in the 'Vette and tore ass however far the tank would carry her. She could get that big, hairy dog and name him Bukowski and never cut his balls.

All because she left me for the right reasons.

It wouldn't be long before the halfway house found out that dead Tony was my boss, and they were going to have a bunch of questions about that. But I would worry about that later. For now, Cassidy was on the open road, and I was with Mom Jon, pushing her wheelchair out of the hospital.

Once we were a block away, I stopped and called Python Wally, begging him for a ride. I bribed him by offering to make the next gruesome batch of the ol' Almighty myself. He couldn't imagine an evening clean of meatloaf and immediately agreed, said he'd grab us in twenty.

Out of nowhere, Mom Jon asked me, "What happened to the waterslides?"

"Do you mean Slide City?"

"I remember living with them."

"I'm glad that you're remembering," I said, but I was tired of her plucking things out of the darkness that weren't me.

"I want to be at the slides again," she said.

She was in a wheelchair, and I was in an electric chair.

She could keep sentencing me to death, or she could remember me.

She suddenly looked concerned. "How did we do that?" she asked.

"Do what?"

"I don't understand how we traveled back in time," she said.

I didn't know what to do. Was I supposed to correct her, or was I supposed to play along? I didn't want to upset her, wanted to keep her calm, keep her talking, keep her brain working out.

"You are Mom Jon," I said, "and I'm your friend."

Right as I said that she squinted up at me from the wheelchair, studying my face. "You came and got me out of the darkness, right?"

"You got me out of the darkness, too," I said, "but then you left me in it again."

"Why did I do that?" she asked, and it was so strange to hear her ask the question that clanked around my body every night after lights out in Quentin. It was a phenomenon and a maze. Many days in there, the years didn't feel like the punishment. No, the wondering, the conjecture, the hole of never knowing *why*. And now we were two people who would never know the truth, or maybe we would with time.

"Hopefully, we'll find out together," I said.

"And my dirt stage," she said, "I brought it with me."

"Brought it where?"

"Slide City. It's with the boy's guitar," she said.

Every berserker and bloodhound in me roared: "What boy?"

"I left it on the stage," she said.

"Can you tell me what boy?"

"It's waiting for him."

"Is James his name?"

"It will need new strings."

"That's my name, Mom Jon. I'm James."

"He'll be so thrilled to get it back," she said, "to be playing again."

Baldr, that god who gave us light and joy, put on quite a show inside my body. “Can you bring me to his guitar?” I asked her.

“They’re looking after it.”

“Who?”

“The ghosts,” she said.

I BARELY RECOGNIZED Python Wally without his big beard in a hairnet. "Do I want to know what this is about?" he asked after he picked us up.

"It's about the woman I was looking for," I said, motioning to Mom Jon in his back seat. "We need to go to Slide City."

Mom Jon dozed. We were dealing with a tangle of cars as the lanes merged on the freeway, clocking in at about fifteen miles an hour, taillights and horns, commuter garden party.

"So how is your fuckup in progress going anyway?" said Python.

"It's wrapping up," I said. "Only one real loose end."

"What's that?"

"That man who got stabbed with the sword and burned up. He was my boss."

That made Python Wally howl with laughter. "I'm sure you weren't involved."

"I certainly didn't stab him or start the fire, if that's what you're saying."

"That is quite a loose end," he said.

"And that woman they think did it is my girlfriend." I paused, pondered. "I think. I mean, we never put a label on it."

"So two loose ends," he said.

"One and a half."

"My advice is to get another job today, tomorrow at the latest," he said. Someone cut in front of Wally in their pickup, and it took effort to dam his rage. Python turned red, only for a second, then did some box breathing, calming down. Then he said to me, "The legal system is so fucked up and behind, they may never even know you worked for him."

"I doubt even the State of California is that stupid."

That made him laugh even harder. "The State of California," Python Wally said, "couldn't find its avocados with both hands."

"I hope you're right," I said.

"I'm glad you found her," Python said. "I'm glad you want to write those songs. They sound like purpose, like you found yours."

He was right: Songs could keep me alive. But that wasn't the whole story. I had to tell him the other part, too. "She doesn't know who I am," I said. "She doesn't remember me."

And now he laughed the hardest of all. I understood his position, though I didn't like it. Sometimes, you were so fucked, you had to laugh. He woke Mom Jon from her nap, and she said to somebody who wasn't there, "Only a peach margarita for me, thanks," and fell right back asleep.

All the cars had successfully been herded onto the bridge now, and we were doing fifty, finally getting on track, finally on our way.

"If it makes you feel any better," Python Wally said to me, "you're a very forgettable person."

ᛗ

We pulled into Slide City. Wally was gonna wait in the car, gave me forty-five minutes to be back or he would leave me there.

Mom Jon was still too weak to walk, and I pushed her in the wheelchair through the parking lot. Obviously, she couldn't climb the fence, so I told her to wait while I went in first. I announced my presence loudly and walked with my hands over my head, in case any of Val's sentries had itchy trigger fingers on their machine guns.

It turned out that the padlock on the chain-link fence belonged to Val and the gang, so they gave me the key, and now I pushed Mom Jon's wheelchair on the decks, past all the ragged patio furniture and empty pools. I peeked in the one where Cassidy and I had stood on the clockwork heart. One week: That was all the time I got with Cassidy. I wanted to be the kind of person who could appreciate what they got without whining for more, but I didn't know how, not with her. It wasn't every day that a woman without eyebrows shit in a fish tank and taught you to drive, showed you that it was possible to get less rusty at being alive, right up until her gun went off.

Val and the gang all cheered and clapped when they saw Mom Jon being wheeled toward their community. "Do I know these people?" Mom Jon said to me before we were in earshot, and I said, "They're your friends," and she said, "Why do they look like hobos?" and she was right: off-the-grid survivalists were *Mad Max* chic, and I didn't tell her this, and I'm embarrassed to say it to you, but fine, fuck it, I had an urge to sing "(I've Had) the Time of My Life" because I got her out of the darkness, yes, and I brought her home.

M

Mom Jon and me. After I carried her up all the stairs. We stood at the top of the waterslide. The one that had the waterlogged teenage ghosts stashed way down its throat. We stood at the mouth. You couldn't see anything inside.

"I already went in there," I said. "I didn't see my guitar or your dirt stage."

"You didn't go far enough," she said. "Come on."

She got down on all fours and crawled into the dark tube, and I hunched over and followed her down.

We heard a greeting from the ghosts, a low frequency, snoring.

"It's just me!" Mom Jon called to them.

The voices grew excited, gasping.

"Well, I'm off drugs, if that's what you're asking," she said to them.

Now they sounded like icicles tinkling in a breeze.

"He's with me," she said, and then she said to me, though I couldn't see her face as we continued to crawl, "They've been protecting the stage. Ghosts are incredible guard dogs."

And with that, the voices roared, a gruff warbling weather system.

I didn't speak ghost. Maybe their climate was agreeing with Mom Jon; they were proper guards. Mom Jon was cool as the other side of the pillow as we inched deeper into the dry esophagus. So if she thought the ghosts were allies, who was I to pretend to know more?

Or it could be that, like when I'd been near them with Cassidy, they hissed a windstorm to scare us away. *This is our homeland,* they told us. *You cross into our borders, then we go to war*. It was always problematic trying to read the minds of ghosts.

Mom Jon and I reached that line that Cassidy and I didn't cross before, an imaginary boundary that meant entry into their world.

"We're almost there," said Mom Jon, pushing on, crawling on all fours, a burrowing woman working her way to her dirt stage, to the home she took with her when they knocked the building down. She scooted on the dry slide, and I was right behind her, no place I'd rather be. The waterlogged teenage ghosts were buzzing now, a whirring hard drive. They weren't getting any louder, any more agitated, as we neared their castle walls. They weren't scared of us, that was for sure.

"Okay," Mom Jon said, stopping. "Here."

I peeked over her shoulder, and sure enough, there was the dirt stage, all eighteen inches of it.

"I couldn't bring the whole thing," she said.

"What you got is great," I said.

"I must've liked you."

"Yes, we loved each other."

"And you sang Iggy Pop."

"All the time."

"And you're the boy."

"Yes."

"You want to know the answer to the question: Where is your guitar?"

"Yes, please," I said.

"But I'll only know if you're the boy if you go up there and sing." And she pointed to the other side of the dirt stage. At first, I couldn't make out the black guitar case, camouflaged in the dark. I climbed over the tiny dirt stage, threw the case opened, held the happy monster. I brought it up and let its body touch my forehead. I held it there. We had a private conversation that doesn't concern you.

Then the ghosts began to growl, low at first, but revving up on the quick. I gazed in their direction, half expecting to see ghosts with wet animal eyes down deeper in the throat. But I couldn't see anything except black.

"They want to hear you play," Mom Jon said.

"They do?"

"Yeah."

And I said, "I don't have a cord to plug in my guitar," and she said, "Yes, that's true," and I said, "I don't have an amp," and she said, "Yes, that's true, too," and I said, "If I don't have an amp, nobody will hear me play," and she said, "I will, and they will, and you will, and that's enough," and I said, "It is?" and she said, "Get on that dirt stage and play," and I said, "I can't stand on the stage in a tube slide because I'm too tall," and she said, "Jesus, just fucking sit on the stage and play already," and I crashed my ass down on the dirt stage, and I sat crisscross applesauce, and I played a chord, and the instrument was in the key of Mangled, but I had a good ear, found E, and tuned the rest of the strings to that, felt the pinch of the metal wires across fingertips that had sloughed their calluses, lost their dexterity, clumsy and slow, like washed-up prizefighters.

I hit a few more chords, waking my hands, remembering.

Mom Jon was on one side of the stage.

The ghosts were on the other.

And when I started playing, Mom Jon said my name, and then she said, "I remember you!"

She knew me.

Can you understand how hearing this was more thrilling than skydiving? Monkeys didn't need to see the sky if their mothers remembered who they were.

She came back.

I got her back.

We were back together.

My life was usually about losing people. People loved leaving me. The most recent case was Cassidy, whom I knew for such a short span of time that her eyebrows didn't have a chance to grow back. From when I first saw her through those balloons in the lobby, from her offering me all those half-frozen shrimp, from her teaching me to drive in Slide City's parking lot, from dancing together right after she shot Ced's dad, Cassidy had become one of my favorite people. They say nothing bonded you to your friends more than shared history, but that didn't mean you needed a lot of it; it just meant you needed the right history.

Hopefully, she drove the 'Vette to a new secret, fulfilling life.

Hopefully, she was living the shit out of it.

As I played my guitar in the tube, I didn't yet know I wouldn't hear from the corporate investors again until that night in the future, on that dirt road in New Mexico. In fact, I never once went back to Unit 12, the place I theoretically owned. They gave it to me, and for five thousand reasons, I couldn't live there, the most pressing being that they'd already come inside to kill Tony. Sure, I could change the locks, but how could I ever relax enough to sleep? I was probably on the hook for thousands of dollars in property tax, but I didn't care. That was for the future, and I was at peace in the present, sitting on a dirt stage in a waterslide, playing the happy monster, couldn't stop, wouldn't, didn't know how . . .

I had a rabid fan base of waterlogged teenage ghosts.

I had Mom Jon, and she smiled at me.

She remembered me.

She knew exactly who I was.

PART 4

THE MAN IN THE ATTIC

(BACK TO THE PRESENT)

ONCE UPON A TIME, there were two fools in the desert, twacked on acid and malt liquor. They stumbled down a dirt road at sunrise, speaking in hallucinogenically hemorrhaging language. One was named Got Jokes; the other, Dusty. Both talked like a stroke fucked an overdose.

"For instance, a firing squad," Dusty said to Got Jokes. "We can all agree that would be over-the-top. I'm not saying play Uno and, if you lose, face the firing squad."

"That'd be nuts."

"Of course. Gross. I'm saying inject the game with some consequence."

"Totally," Got Jokes said. "Give Uno a nitrous blast."

"Baste that fucker with some life sauce." Then Dusty pointed at his ears, the drugs fluffing his perceptions. He said to Got Jokes, "If you really listen, you can hear the whole system, man. It's ugly-ass music, but it's all there if you aim your ears right. Watch me! I'm listening now. Watch, bitch!"

Got Jokes, for some reason, whispered like a scared child. "What are you hearing?"

"An atom's heartbeat."

"No shit?"

"An amoeba sneezing."

"Amoebas sneeze?"

"I hear how sunlight sounds," said Dusty. "I can hear the chatter inside a diner that only serves meals to the dead."

I'd roused the fools from the Reliant's back seat, right after Princess Di shot out our lights and left us. Already cranky and beginning their comedown, they complained like brats being dragged from bed before school, so I helped them to their feet a tad violently, and we set off walking in the desert morning. I filled the philosophers in on the spike strip, the guns, the stolen guitar, Cassidy. They marveled about how drastically our lives could change while we closed our eyes, how we could miss everything. Now that I was out of Quentin, I wanted to turn myself into an insomniac. Wanted to be awake for as much of my life as I could. During my time in prison, I turned off most parts of myself, like the lights at Jacques' place. All I left on inside me was one single bulb from the fridge.

Now, the fools walked behind us—the *three* of us. Trick Wilma, Cassidy, and me. We three hoofed in a line in the direction of the club, going deeper down the desert road, watching the sun shake the cobwebs out, loosen up its muscles to scorch.

The three of us didn't know what to say to one another, and so we all moved silently in a straight line, me in the middle. Our soundtrack was the crunch of boots and the fools' acid dreck behind us.

"Isn't she supposed to be filling us in?" Trick asked me. "That's what that Princess Di dick said to us."

"What do you know, Cassidy?" I said.

Cassidy didn't have the Beetlejuice mask on anymore, but she was still dressed like him, in a black-and-white-striped suit. Her hands remained zip-tied in front of her. "I know I want these off," she said, shaking the zip tie at us.

"Keep dreaming," Trick said.

"What can you tell us about them, Cassidy?" I said.

"This is for what we did," she said, "the Sid & Nancy. We have to work off all the property damage we caused."

"What's the Sid & Nancy?" Trick said.

"After all this time? Now they come for us?" I asked Cassidy. "Why now?"

"I wondered that, too," she said, "and they told me that it took over a year to get everything ready for what they want to do."

"What do they want to do?"

"We find that out at the club."

"How did they get to you?" I asked.

"Beats me. I was at a bar. Somebody drugged my drink. I don't know who did it. I woke up today in New Mexico, dressed like this."

"Do you know what we're walking into at this club?" I said to her.

"I only know that we get our marching orders there. We have to go."

Trick stopped and squared right up to Cassidy, who didn't budge back at all. These were two Valkyries, battle-tested, sizing each other up. Instinctually, the fools behind us dissolved their huddle around our clog, one of them passing us on either side, and then they came back together right in stride, like they'd practiced it a hundred times.

"I don't believe you," Trick said, her face inches from Cassidy's. "In fact, I don't know who you even fucking are."

"I'm a murderer," said Cassidy, "and you're too close to me."

"Who'd you kill?"

"Ask him," Cassidy said, pointing at me. "He was there."

"Was he?" Trick asked, then to me: "Were you?"

"Yeah, he saw the whole thing," said Cassidy. "He was doing something romantic for me."

"Murder does sound romantic," Trick said.

"You had to be there," Cassidy said.

Their bodies didn't move, but their eyes were already using fists. I'd be lying if I said that I wasn't enjoying watching their pissing contest, and I dug being around Cassidy again, even if the way she parachuted back into my life was a complete mind-fuck time machine.

Here, offered the vulgar machine, *let's reanimate all your old ache.*

"So they drugged you and took you?" Trick asked Cassidy.

"Yeah."

"When?"

"Yesterday."

"From where?"

"Eastern Washington."

"Did you hear them say anything?"

"They mostly made me wear headphones that blasted loud music."

"I wouldn't believe this bitch with a polygraph shoved up her ass," Trick said to me.

Trick was right; we couldn't trust her.

"That's not how polygraphs work," Cassidy said.

"You're in on this," Trick said. "I can smell it."

"I'm not in on it."

"What concerns me, Cassidy," Trick said, "is what else might be waiting for us at the club besides instructions. It was Cassidy, right? That's your name?"

"Yup, that's me: Cassidy, the cold-blooded murderer."

"A zip-tied, cold-blooded murderer," Trick said.

"And you are?"

"Not zip-tied," said Trick, "and not talking to you anymore." Trick broke the stare, stayed right in Cassidy's face but swiveled her head toward me, saying, "She was with them when we first saw her. How do we know she's not still with them? Shit, she might be *them*."

My body wanted to immediately reject this idea of Cassidy being *them*. It was a flavor that hit my stomach and made me want to puke. She was half of the Sid & Nancy. We caused all that mayhem together. She was supposed to be one of *us*, not one of *them*. But she'd been on the lam, and I didn't know her anymore. It was possible that they had gotten to her, and she was setting us up, as much as I didn't want to believe it.

Death wasn't the end game. Otherwise, why not just take us out on the road when they shot out the Reliant's headlights before? There was something else they wanted, and it revolved around repaying this debt.

"You could just ask me if I'm them," said Cassidy to Trick, "and you're still standing too fucking close to me."

"I'll move, if that's what you want," Trick said, taking a couple of steps back right to me and wrapping herself in my arms. "Thanks," she said to Cassidy, "for the good idea. If you don't mind, we need to have a private fucking conversation."

Cassidy started walking toward the club. She passed the dawdling fools, who were inching now, staring straight up into the sky.

"So they lured us here with a fake gig," Trick said to me.

"Yup, the road's secluded. They hunted us."

"What do you think they want?" Trick said.

"We need to go to the club to find out," I said.

"Oh, cool, let's fall right in their trap."

"I'll go."

"And you want me to stay with her and the acid podcasters?!"

"I want to protect you," I said.

"That's sweet," said Trick, "and also fuck you."

On a cactus about fifteen feet away, as the morning brightened around us, sitting right on the cactus's head, there was one of my father's glass birds. The sun cut through its gleaming green body. In case you don't know or remember, my father was a famous glass-blowing Viking artist in the mother country. He made his name blowing fire into these birds and bringing them to life. This one now joined me for moral support, and me and this bird, we both knew that the club was the only way to learn what this debt was and how to pay it.

At the same time, we both knew, the bird and me, that Trick was right: We were walking into a trap.

I called to Cassidy, who rejoined us. I told the two women that I'd clear the club of any danger. They didn't want to stay behind together. They'd done plenty of "bonding." I won the argument by pointing out that the fools were on acid and shouldn't come to the club. People were rarely helpful while swinging from that carnival chandelier. And if the fools were going to be left behind, they needed supervision. In their current condition, it was likely one might try to kiss a rattlesnake, and since Cassidy's zip tie wasn't coming off yet, the fools needed two-handed Trick to take the lead.

Yup, Trick and Cassidy, hanging out in the desert without me. Here I was, a man getting ready to storm into battle, and yet I found myself thinking, *Will they talk about me while I'm gone?*

The glass bird cawed now, growing impatient.

I understood; it was time.

I said to Trick, "I'll be back and I'll be safe," and she said, "Okay, I'll try not to kill her while you're gone," and I said, "I love you," and she said, "I love you, too," and I set off running down the dirt road. With each stride, my body sloshed, and my Vikings felt a rollicking sea under their longship, and they adored the challenge of a tussling ocean trying to slow them down, pounding them with rain and waves, and the men howled in the moonlight, and they rowed and they rowed and they rowed . . .

I felt every splash of lawlessness, heard the chants of dead warriors. These were berserkers, after all, and they didn't know table manners or the *Mona Lisa*, and they thought opera was how rich people complained. They didn't need to be sophisticated, only needed to dream of a Valhalla that was so majestic that going there tempted them as much as staying alive. So they transformed into wolves.

I was happy to have them along.

Them and the glass bird.

We neared the rise in the road—*we* meaning the berserkers, the bird, and me. Obviously. And while we couldn't spy the club yet, I started hearing it. There was music playing. Rock and roll. A shitkicker.

Soon, we'd be able to peek over the rise.

Soon, we'd be able to see.

ALL THE LIGHTS WERE ON, both inside and outside the club. The parking lot was completely empty of cars, and there was a marquee that only said my name. Not the band's. No. Just: SAINT THE TERRIFYING. The music I'd heard only in ambient growls was Butthole Surfers, screeching their record *Independent Worm Saloon*. Right now, the song was wondering who was in their room last night, and I took that as my cue to investigate.

I hiked fast from the rise to the club, the hitter-quitter in my hand and berserkers in my blood. Under different circumstances, these gritty gross clubs that allowed our gritty gross songs to exist in public were some of my favorite places. They smelled like mattresses soaked in beer piss, but they kept our music alive. For perhaps the first time in my life, I approached such a place with mistrust—call it, even, reasonable fear.

I stomped my combat boot through the front door. Sent it from the hinges. Held the hitter-quitter up like a battle ax, keeping my back near one of the walls so nobody could get the jump on me from behind. There was a big bar running down the opposite wall of where I slowly walked. The back of the club was its stage. But that bar across the room . . . I couldn't see what was behind it, didn't know if there were any people hidden.

Whether they were there wasn't the point. The point was they *may* be there, and I needed to hasten their reveal. It was time for some re-decorating.

I snuck to the nearest pool table, grabbed a billiard ball, threw it against the liquor bottles behind the bar, shattering a bunch; threw another one, detonating, and anybody back there was getting drenched in booze and their skin was being stung by these bottle-wasps spitting their stingers; threw four more balls until the majority of the bottles were memories, and I sprinted across the room, leaped over the bar. I screamed with the hitter-quitter cocked to slam heads. But there wasn't anybody there.

That didn't mean I was alone. There was a dark doorway by the stage, one that led to the back, the offices, the green room, and from that shadowed maw I heard a war cry, a man's yelling voice, and he said to me, "You coming or what?"

I had to assume there was more with him, had to assume that the hitter-quitter might require reinforcements for the next phase of this. Back in the New York hard-core scene of the early '80s, they'd called a pool ball in the toe of a sock a "madball," and so now I exited my boot and took off a sock, tied the shoe back up, loaded up the nine ball, and I had a swinging madball in one mitt and the hitter-quitter in the other.

I worried, however, that might not be enough, worried that other warriors had tucked themselves away in various crannies around the club, and I'd be operating at such a disadvantage that I was cosigning my own beating, own death. To those worries I replied, *Let's fucking go.*

"I'll be right there, sweetheart," I said to the voice. "Go ahead and slip into something you're comfortable getting bloodstains on."

There was a book of matches behind the bar, and suddenly, the glass bird appeared, perched on the cash register.

"Maybe their village burns," I said, and the bird cawed a melody of approval, so I struck a match, tossed it into a pool of alcohol, and in seconds, the wall behind the bar wiggled with flames.

Twenty seconds later, it raged and smoked, and the voice who lived in the cave called to me, "Is something burning?"

"I'm cooking you dinner, darling," I said.

I swung the madball, held the hitter-quitter up like a sword.

Now I heard a couple of voices back there, whispering, confused.

A beat.

Me staring at the mouth of their darkened cave, hearing their pack quietly strategizing.

Then the infantry barreled in. Three of them. Not huge, but not small. Six feet tall, say. Moving like they were trained. Running toward me.

One had a hockey mask on.

One had a Freddy Krueger mask.

One wore Ghost Face from the *Scream* movies.

They carried blades, but with the length of my long arms and my long-distance weapons, they'd never get close enough to stab me. The times I'd fought more than one man at once, my secret was always attacking the ones I wasn't making eye contact with, so I stared at the one in the middle. I'd get off the center line, cut an angle, make them move their feet from side to side so their weight wasn't steady.

I swung the madball at the one on the left, popped it right on his temple, then I ducked to evade returning fire, bobbed over to the other side, and smashed the one on the right across the knee with the hitter-quitter. He fell and I kicked him in the face, and at the same time, I threw the wrecking ball sock toward the face of the one who'd been in the middle, not to hurt him necessarily, though that could be a happy by-product. I threw it simply to make him draw his hands up to protect his face, which left his torso unprotected, meaning I had a clean line to his liver, landing the end of the hitter-quitter right on the fragile organ, and in eight seconds, these three were on the ground.

My joy reached its cruising altitude. My joy could fly across the country without any fuel.

I kicked one of them in his hockey mask.

I kicked Freddy Krueger right in his burned temple.

I kicked Ghost Face in his head so hard that his mask flew off. A young cat. Twenty and change. He was unconscious from the boot. I was what you might call a generous face kicker. A generous face kicker in a burning bar. I didn't want any of their faces to feel left out.

Butthole Surfers were still yelling from the speakers. They were gonna see this through with me.

"How many other heads are back there?" I said, pointing to the darkened door that led to the back of the club. Their injuries made small talk hard. Then the phone behind the bar rang. The glass bird and I looked at each other. Neither of us was expecting a call.

The fire spread to the ceiling and moved down the wall. The floor behind the bar also erupted, and so I stretched the phone cord, took the remainder of the call sitting on a stool at a bar that was on fire. I picked up the phone but didn't say hello.

The stage was already starting to catch, too. It was weird watching an empty stage burn. Felt sacrilegious. Like I was doing the wrong thing, and maybe I was.

"He's waiting for you in the attic," the guy on the phone said to me. It was Princess Di's voice.

"I thought you were just a humble courier," I said.

"I dabble."

"A jack-of-all-trades."

"You have to hear what he has to say."

"The building's on fire."

"I know that. You don't think we're watching everything?"

"The building's on fire."

"Then you should probably hurry."

"Or I let him burn up," I said.

"Then you'll never find her."

Her: What did he mean by that?

"Who?" I asked.

"You lied to me earlier," Princess Di said, "and that hurts my feelings."

"When did I lie?"

"You said your guitar was what you loved the most. But that's not true. *Who*, Saint. Who do you love more than anything?"

Trick. I'd left Trick behind. With only twacked Dusty and Got Jokes. Only with zip-tied Cassidy.

I didn't know which path to take. I looked to the bar's front door: Should I run back to where I'd left Trick back in the desert?

I took a gander at the bar's burning ceiling, toward its attic: Should I run up to where I'd meet the man and get some answers?

Or should I step outside and wait, watch the whole building burn until the mystery man had to flee the attic?

Sometimes, survival really came down to picking the right answer to a multiple-choice test.

Princess Di said into the phone, "It's getting hot in here, Saint. So what's it going to be?"

I SPED BACKSTAGE, the hitter-quitter and madball ready if anyone jumped out from a corner. I moved down the hall toward the office, saw the hatch in the ceiling, the way to enter the attic. I pulled the string, and a ladder dropped down.

Smoke wafted down the hall.

This part of the building wasn't burning yet, but it was only a matter of minutes. That was how fires worked, those gluttonous destroyers. Fires were what people didn't have the courage to be: honest in their havoc. Still, we all melted the same way.

All the lights in the club had blazed outside and downstairs, but as I worked my way up the attic's ladder, this space was utterly dark. I couldn't see three feet in front of me. At the top, I fumbled with a few close beams, hunting for a light switch. Found it and lights came on, barely. It was dim.

Most of the attic wasn't finished, meaning that there wasn't a floor. It was mostly two-by-sixes forming a sort of rigid spiderweb, and between these pieces of frame, there was only the pink pubes of insulation.

Also, a small couch, and sitting on it, an oversized laptop. From the screen, there was a smiling face staring at me, welcoming me.

This was a man with a powdered face, who wore a Mozart wig. "I hear we don't have much time," he said. "I hear you lit the place on fire," and he erupted in peals of laughter.

I was kneeling on the ladder's top step, hadn't entered the attic in earnest. "Who are you?"

"I'm a scientist."

"What's your name?"

"You're my lab rat."

"The fuck I am."

"That makes forty-two of our properties that you've destroyed," he said. "I'll add it to your debt. Which is why you're here."

I'd never talked to a computer on a couch in an attic in a burning club before. And I didn't like his smile, let alone the Mozart wig. "How would I pay my debt if your friends downstairs had killed me?" I said.

"Oh, they weren't going to end your life. I'm merely evaluating you."

I climbed off the ladder's top rung, balanced on one of the attic's two-by-sixes on my knees. "Evaluating me?"

"Collecting data on my lab rat," he said, "seeing what you're capable of doing. At worst, they would've injured you, taken you prisoner, brought you to me."

"No one's bringing me to you."

"If they can't," he said, "you can."

"I can bring me to you?" I asked the powdered man on the laptop. My knees ached on the two-by-six, so I stood up, balanced on it, needed to hunch over because I was too tall for this attic.

"I have something remarkable planned for you," he said. "You're going to love the experiment."

"The experiment?"

"Congratulations on embarking on this career opportunity with us, Saint," he said. "You're getting in on the ground floor of an exciting enterprise. Come over here. Sit with me."

I tightroped the frame and made my way to the couch, sat next to the computer like we were two friends watching the Super Bowl.

"Our company has recently bought an authentic Mississippi riverboat," he said. "We had it loaded on several planes and rebuilt on the Yangtze River. It is a new casino that we want to have an American rock and roll look. As of right now, your band is gainfully employed aboard the ship as the house band."

"Where is this ship?"

"Yichang."

"Where's that?"

"China."

It was beginning to get very smoky in the attic. The fire would blaze in this part of the club soon.

"You'll play six days a week," he said.

"Why would we do that?" I said.

From the hatch in the floor, the first ripples of fire. Like it was walking up the stairs. Like it was making an entrance, that pyro diva.

"Trick Wilma has already left for China," he said. "We scooped her up while you were busy tussling with my colleagues. She'll travel with us. Your flight information is back in the Reliant, along with your guitar we borrowed temporarily. Everyone in your party has clean passports. You start in three days."

I stood up from the couch and balance-walked the frame toward the window. It was way over a hundred degrees up there. My eyes were watering, and I suddenly had a huge headache.

The fire had reached the couch, reached the laptop. The man's face was on fire.

"If you don't show," he said, "you understand she'll experience consequences."

"I'll show," I said, "and I hope we meet in person."

"We are meeting in person right now," said the on-fire, powdered face on the computer, and busted up in hysterics. It took a beat to compose himself, then he said, "But if you meant on the ship, yes, of course we will meet there. I have all kinds of experiments lined up for you, Saint, made just for you," and he laughed again. I was tired of being laughed at by a burning laptop. "You all will live on the boat," he said. "You won't leave it. I own you until your debt is paid."

"Oh, you own me?" I asked, like my ancestors talking to a Christian. When would people learn that we were untrainable?

"I wish I could stay and chat, but my motherboard is being fried," he said. "Ouch, I can feel my processors sizzle. Uh-oh, there goes my microchip."

Then the laptop's screen and speakers bent, melted, and the powdered man in the attic disappeared.

I WAS OUT THE WINDOW, off the roof, on the ground, running as fast as I could back to where I'd left them, assuming the worst, that the man in the attic had told the truth, and Trick was gone. We had three days to get to China or he'd hurt her. My feet pounded on the dirt, and I was almost to the rise in the road, and right on the other side was where I'd last seen them. I smelled like the fire, and I smelled like the man in the attic.

I moved up and over the rise, and there they were, Cassidy standing and pacing with her zip-tied hands and Beetlejuice threads, while Dusty and Got Jokes were both lying down, squinting up at the morning sky. The sun showed its mean streak as it stared back. All you had to do was gaze straight at that apex predator, then shut your eyes, and the backs of your lids glittered with sparks.

Trick wasn't there, of course; the man in the attic wasn't lying about that. I didn't figure they'd hurt her. There would be no advantage in that, if they really thought they were lining us up to be their house band. So I tried not to let my imagination form films of punishment and spite. I tried to believe that they wouldn't lay a hand on her, and if I learned otherwise, I would be bringing the Old World with me.

I walked close to Cassidy, barely a foot apart. I was livid about Trick, sure, but at the same time, I was relieved to see that Cassidy hadn't been roughed up.

"Are you okay?" I asked her.

"There was nothing I could have done," Cassidy said to me. "Too many of them."

"Are you okay?" I asked again.

"Not at all."

"What did they say?"

"Not one word," said Cassidy. "They screeched up and grabbed her. She hit one in the ear and kicked another in the balls before they threw her in the back seat."

That sounded like my Valkyrie.

I studied Dusty and Got Jokes stretched out on the dirt road, stargazing in the desert morning. "Did they do anything to help?"

"I'm not even sure they noticed."

"They're on a lot of acid."

"They'll get sunburned soon," Cassidy said.

Right then, Got Jokes said to Dusty, "I'm familiar with the mainstream constellations, but do you know any obscure ones?"

"Not really."

"I told you," said Got Jokes, "that I don't know *any*—so because I won't know if you're lying to me, you should make them up."

"You want me to lie to you about the stars?" Dusty asked.

"I think that sounds epic," Got Jokes said.

"Normally, people don't want to be lied to."

"Normally," Got Jokes echoed before drifting off. Their distraction slowed me down and somehow calmed me. My adrenaline was dumping from the fire, and I needed to breathe, to think. These couriers had had me on my heels all morning. And while it was true that Trick wasn't there anymore, I could hear her voice crackle in my skull: *Don't be dumb, don't trust Cassidy, don't risk it . . .*

"Do you have any idea what they want from us?" I asked Cassidy.

"I don't even know who *they* are."

"We have to go to Yichang. China."

"What, when?"

"Basically now."

"I can't," she said. "I'm wanted for murder. I'll get popped at the airport."

"They left us clean passports."

That made her scoff: "Oh, and I'm supposed to take their word for it? What if that's their plan? They want me to get arrested."

If she was in on it, Cassidy was a magnificent actor. You could argue that I wanted to give her the benefit of the doubt, and so it was easy for me to fall for her charade. But she genuinely looked panicked that she might get caught going through security.

"I met someone at the club," I said. "We pay our Sid & Nancy debt over there on a riverboat."

"I'm not going to China," Cassidy said.

"We have to."

"I'm not."

"You are."

"Have fun on your trip," she said.

Dusty pointed to a part of the bright morning sky where we could see zero stars. "We can start this with an easy one," Dusty said to Got

Jokes, "because that constellation is called Mia Zapata. Can you see her smiling at us?"

The singer of the Gits had been murdered in Seattle at twenty-seven years old, so it was bliss to imagine her huge face in the sky, blazing with the heat of stars.

I couldn't trust Cassidy, and she couldn't trust the clean passports, and I thought, *In one way or another, we are all seeing imaginary constellations.*

I WANTED to spring Cassidy from her zip tie as an act of good faith. Not being trusting. Not being dumb. Just trying to make her ease up some. If I showed some grace, maybe we'd be able to talk about China. My fingers grazed her zip tie. "Let's get you out of that."

"Do you have a knife on you?"

"Zip ties are only hard to get out of if you're the one wearing them. Here. Watch." There was a cactus a few feet away from where we stood, and I plucked one lone needle from it and used it to spring the snap joint, and the zip tie's teeth opened right up.

"Aren't you a regular Boy Scout?" said Cassidy.

"Viking," I said.

She rubbed her wrists, bending and flexing them.

I wanted to be away from the acid astronomers, and so I said, "Let's take a walk together." Then I spoke to Got Jokes and Dusty, not that our daytime stargazers were paying any attention to us: "Hey, we'll be back in ten minutes," and Dusty pointed to another patch of sky and said, "That constellation's called Darby Crash."

Cassidy and I took off. It was already in the high eighties. We wandered into the open desert. Mostly scrub brush, the occasional cactus. The only life around us were the doves zipping. They were the only life we could see. Most animals hid in their holes from that T-rex shining in the sky. From the other side of the rise, you could see smoke wafting from the bones of the burning club.

Cassidy pointed toward the plume. "I see you haven't lost your touch. The Ol' Nancy & . . . Nancy."

"Old habits," I said.

"I'm one of your old habits."

"You were more than a habit, Cassidy."

"But you kicked me cold turkey," she said, "when I left."

I understood what she meant by calling us a habit and me going clean, but it didn't feel like kicking. Withdrawal was urgent and flagrant and battering. Kicking Cassidy wasn't that fast. After she bolted, I trained myself not to wonder about her. I unplugged all those questions from their amplifiers, and once they were turned down to whispers, I learned to live with those grumbles. And now here she was, raised from the dead. Baldr brought her back.

My father had made me read an Icelandic saga about Baldr. It was impossible to hurt him physically; he was impervious to harm—and because of that, the other gods amused their bored god-brains by throwing things at Baldr, gashing him, slicing him, and watching him heal right up.

Even the gods couldn't help themselves: We all wanted to see someone else's agony.

"Have you been happy?" I said to Cassidy.

She startled, blinking eyes, like I'd jumped out and scared her. But we were in the open desert, and there was no place to hide. "Of course not," she said. "Give me one good reason to be happy!"

Maybe we stood under one of Dusty's imaginary constellations, this one named after Dee Dee Ramone.

In the distance, a roadrunner lived up to the hype, racing across the desert at such speed you assumed it was late for work and needed to make rent.

"I don't mean today," I said to Cassidy. "It's been a shit-casserole morning, obviously. I mean in general. Since I saw you last."

Her startled eyes welled with tears. "Let me answer you with a little story," she said.

"IT'S A STORY," Cassidy said to me, "about a sad hero named me. Somebody who can only earn money under the table on account of a murder charge. You get it, right? Employers get a little squirrelly once they find out you blew a guy's chest open. I guess it makes them wonder if you're trustworthy. What can you do in these can't-fight-city-hall loops? Because of these stacked decks, our hero scrapes by in restaurant jobs, staying in a town for a few weeks, maybe a month, and then moving on. She can't make friends. Friends ask questions. Friends want to get to know you. And she can't have that. God. Friends are just witnesses that haven't turned on you yet. It's a toxic way to think and a toxic way to live—and that's the only thing I've been allowed to do, to be. I can't make friends and I can't stay anyplace for long. I . . . drift. Okay, more cities, more towns, more odd jobs, more empty hours. I started drinking again. But no drugs. I always worried that taking a drink would lead me back to the pipe, and it might someday, but not yet. I sip wine out of coffee cups. Sometimes, I even drink my red wine on the rocks. I know. Déclassé. Hooch on the rocks. Welcome to the trailer park, where the houses have wheels and the cars don't. So sue me: I like the way the ice tinkles in the mug, and I double-like cold red wine. Call me a heathen. No one ever said Cassidy had class.

It bothered me a lot at first, that I was drinking again. Pretty soon, it's just back in your life again and feels involuntary. A week goes by or a month. It's really hard to tell. Maybe you get that from your time being in prison. Friday morning leads to Sunday afternoon straight into Wednesday evening. On one such time-busted night—a Thursday in December or a Tuesday in June—there I am, in a new town working at a new restaurant, standing at the new sink as a dishwasher. The hero of the story is doing the goddamn dishes. Wears pink rubber gloves. She'd bought them at a gas station. It was the only color they had, and it was a color I'd never seen rubber gloves come in. Pink. Why would a gas station only have pink rubber gloves? I bought a pair. I bought them and brought them in, because I learned the hard way not to accept the free pair they gave you at these kinds of jobs. That comes-with-the-job pair was a thousand years old and was a shrine to bacteria. The skin between your fingers peeled in worms. So on this one night, she washed dishes at a diner in her gas station pink gloves. It was her fucking birthday. She hated doing the dishes on days that were not her birthday, so I was really letting myself have it in my skull. *Cassidy, you piece of shit.* That old chestnut. That catchy tune we like to sing to ourselves. They say that people should do crossword puzzles to keep their minds sharp, but some of us beat ourselves up instead. Those are our mental exercises. It was a regular pity party at this dishwashing birthday soiree. The hero was mind-your-own-business years old. She would get no cards or gifts. No friends would sing to her. She was going by a fake name anyway, and maybe that would've felt even lonelier, hearing people sing 'Happy Birthday' and call her a fake name. In the pink gloves, her hands were pruned from hours in the bog of water and soap. She held a hefty stack of dirty dishes from the bottom right now. Dinner plates. The shape of a traditional birthday cake. She was going to make sixty dollars on her shift. It was the most awful thing in the world, this birthday cake made of dirty dishes, and she used her pink-gloved and pruned hands to throw the whole stack against the wall. It was the loudest cake she'd ever heard. This cake bothered the customers. This cake made the manager come into the kitchen. Our hero wasn't going to take any shit, so she ran out of the diner, got back to where she was camping. In her tent. Happy birthday to me. She still had on the pink rubber gloves. But she was going to change the story. She was going to change the day. Change the story of the day. She fired up the laptop she'd bought thirdhand and opened an account on an amateur porn site. She was old, but these days, that didn't matter. These days, everyone was somebody's fetish. It wasn't going to feel any worse than washing dishes in a diner on your birthday. You do what you need to do in this life, and if perverts want to pay our hero to jerk off, so be it. Digital romance and capitalism. And it's easy money in a safe environment. I wanted to post my first video before my birthday was over so I could make the story more lucrative. No, this wasn't going to be the day I made sixty dollars washing dishes. This was going to be the day when lonely men sent me hundreds of dollars for doing the most natural thing. And it worked. I made two-twenty that night, and all I had to do was touch myself. So that's what our hero does. That's how she earns her living. And her life isn't happy. Maybe her life is good enough. Honestly, she doesn't allow herself to think much about it. Why does any of it matter? Being alive felt like a trick and a trap. So go ahead and judge our hero, go ahead and judge me. If you think it's worse than washing dishes at a diner on your birthday, you're not masturbating right."

A FEW MORE DOVES shoved through the cloudless sky. We were being scalded one degree at a time. The desert wanted us to know that it hated us, down to the liquid metal in its core, that boiling blood, as our feet crunched on the sand, no plan, no map, no direction. She finished telling her story, and I could see her scars and biases and light. She was the brightest star in the desert right then, and there was nothing the sun could do about it.

I stopped walking, and she did, too. Stood face-to-face.

"Do you really think I could judge you?" I said.

"I hope not," she said, "but hope is for babies."

Another roadrunner tore ass through scrub brush with something limp latched in its beak. The bird braked, and I could see that it held a dead snake. It stood there for a few seconds, then slurped that huge noodle for breakfast and took off running again, like an ambulance with its sirens always wailing.

"If hope's for babies," I said, "let's be babies."

"Well, if I was a fucking baby again," said Cassidy, "for starters, I'd appreciate it more. Is there anything worse than being an adult? These lives of ours are just scams and conspiracy theories. If reincarnation is real, the next time I'm Baby Cassidy, I'm gonna lap up all that importance. Take a lot of baths in the sink. Feast on all the goo-goo ga-ga. Enjoy slurping milk straight from the tap. Gotta enjoy the attention, Baby Cassidy. Soon, you'll grow up to be another working stiff with a UTI."

I put my hand out to her, and she scrunched up her face like, *Huh?* and I said, "Let's have another thirty-second dance," and her face scrunched up even further: *Wait, are you for real?* and I scrunched mine to match: *Just one more, why not?* and she put her hand in mine, and our bodies got close, and her hair smelled like honey, and the cacti looked like stupefied aliens, and Cassidy and I looked like hopeful dancing babies, and this was a thirty-second dance that was going to last at least a hundred years.

"Can I tell you something that's silly and sad?" Cassidy asked me. "I thought we were going to be together. Like . . . for a long time."

"I thought that, too," I said.

"And then I shot him," she said.

We turned in circles in the desert. We were alive and had five senses, yes, and there must have been things happening around us: Hidden in holes, there must have been rattlers wearing Hawaiian shirts, Gila monsters playing beer pong, cottontail rabbits packing their bags for a couple nights in Cabo. But I wasn't aware of anything except this dance.

"But I'm not the only one who wrecked us; you did, too," she said, putting her head on my shoulder. "You did, when you fell in love with her."

Half a mile away, there were two people named Dusty and Got Jokes lying on their backs, stargazing in the morning sky, and here, there were two people dancing, stargazing in another way entirely.

"You really do love her, don't you?" she said.

"I do. That's why I need your help."

"Unless I'm arrested at the airport."

"If they want us to pay our debt, why would they walk you into a charge?"

"Those assholes kept me zip-tied all night in a Beetlejuice costume, so trust is pretty fucking hard to come by."

There it was, trust, that unreasonable knot, that ridiculous maze.

We got this unexpected thirty seconds, and if you added our two dances together, we had a minute, only one minute, to mean something to each other.

"If we don't show," I said to Cassidy, "they'll take it out on Trick."

"If we let them kill her, what are the odds that you and I get back together?"

"Can we not let her die?" I asked.

"I guess," she said, "but that means that our thirty seconds are up," and she took her head off my shoulder, stepped back out of our dance.

There was no such thing as real time when you danced in the desert in the arms of somebody whom Baldr raised from the grave, someone you didn't even know if you could trust. No, in cases like this, time took as long as was needed.

"It's not up yet," I said. "We have five seconds left. Don't worry. I've been counting down, and I'm a very skilled counter."

"I thought you were a baby," she said, "and babies can't count."

I put my palm out again and extended it to her. "Haven't you heard? I'm a genius baby who can already count. I've already got a full ride to Harvard."

She accepted my hand, stepped back into my arms. "Oh shit, it's you! The genius baby full of hope."

"The genius baby full of hope," I said, "who's heading to Harvard."

I was a person, and Cassidy was a person, and you're one, too, and I'm glad you're in this desert, and I'm glad you saw that snake-noodle slurp into the roadrunner's mouth, glad that you knew that Mia Zapata and Darby Crash shined from the sky, and I'm glad you're dancing with us, yes, I'm glad you're in my arms. Did you know that your hair smells like honey, too?

Cassidy smiled up at me. "How much time do we have left?"

I was supposed to be counting down from five, but I didn't remember the next digit. All I could see was a horizon of fives, a fortress, a monolith:

fivefivefivefivefivefivefivefivefivefivefivefivefivefivefivefivefivefivefi
vefivefivefivefivefivefivefivefivefivefivefivefivefivefivefivefivefivefive
fivefivefivefivefivefivefivefivefivefivefivefivefivefivefivefivefivefivefiv
efivefivefivefivefivefivefivefivefivefivefivefivefivefivefivefivefivefivefi
vefivefivefivefivefivefivefivefivefivefivefivefivefivefivefivefivefivefivef
ivefivefivefivefivefivefivefivefivefivefivefivefivefivefivefivefivefivefive
fivefivefivefivefivefivefivefivefivefivefivefivefivefivefivefivefivefivefiv
efivefivefivefivefivefivefivefivefivefivefivefivefivefivefivefivefivefivefi
vefivefivefivefivefivefivefivefivefivefivefivefivefivefivefivefivefivefivef
ivefivefivefivefivefivefivefivefivefivefivefivefivefivefivefivefivefivefive
fivefivefivefivefivefivefivefivefivefivefivefivefivefivefivefivefivefivefiv
efivefivefivefivefivefivefivefivefivefivefivefivefivefivefivefivefivefivefi
vefivefivefivefivefivefivefivefivefivefivefivefivefivefivefivefivefivefivef
ivefivefivefivefivefivefivefivefivefivefivefivefivefivefivefivefivefivefive
fivefivefivefivefivefivefivefivefivefivefivefivefivefivefivefivefivefivefiv
efivefivefivefivefivefivefivefivefivefivefivefivefivefivefivefivefivefivefi
vefivefivefivefivefivefivefivefivefivefivefivefivefivefivefivefivefivefivef
ivefivefivefivefivefivefivefivefivefivefivefivefivefivefivefivefivefivefive

five

"One other thing," Cassidy said. "You're Saint now? That's your new name? And she's called Trick Wilma?"

"Punker names," I said.

"I want one, too."

I didn't even need to think about it. "How about Mad Cassidy?" I asked.

"Mad like pissed," she said, "or mad like crazy?"

"Yes," I said.

We busted up laughing, a couple of dancing babies, a couple of overcome monkeys staring at their first sky, witnesses to the marvelous slop that should have dropped all of us to our knees every day—

"Fuck it," she said, "let's go save your new girlfriend."

This metastasizing wonder, this joy volcano, this awed botulism, this confident trombone, this radioactive epiphany—

I was headed to China to get Trick, and I'd kill anyone in my way.

A war riot chanted in my heart: *Be wild, you're the wolf . . .*